PARTY WIVES

PARTY WIVES

JIM LAYNE

CUTTING EDGE

ISBN-13: 978-1-962896-75-7

Published by
Cutting Edge Books
PO Box 8212
Calabasas, CA 91372
www.cuttingedgebooks.com

CHAPTER ONE

Nora Osborne, sitting on the clubhouse veranda with a Coke, strove for the sense of well-being that, all things considered, she believed should be hers. But for some reason she could not define, she failed to achieve the coveted mood.

Why? she wondered. What ails me anyway? She was genuinely perplexed and more than a little disturbed.

Here she was, still in her twenties—if only for a few months longer—reasonably attractive, the beloved wife of David and basking in the bright glow of his success. Also, she reminded herself, they were residents of an exclusive suburb, the newly accepted members of the country club set, and parents of seven-year-old Louise, now away for the first time at the accepted camp for the young daughters of the Wilshire Heights families who were definitely on their way up.

She was an accomplished hostess. Her tennis was good and now she was taking up golf. She had been asked to become a member of the Garden Club—an invitation that definitely indicated another rung gained on the social ladder. She was becoming active in civic affairs. And since the Osbornes had acquired the house in fashionable Wilshire Heights, their name had begun to appear in the society columns. Barring an unforseeable stroke of bad luck, Dave would soon be a vice-president in the Worden-Forbes Corporation with his future assured. The Great American Dream was becoming a reality for young Mr. and Mrs. David Osborne.

What more could she ask?

Why didn't she then—for heaven's sake—have that sense of well-being? Wasn't she snobbish enough to enjoy her new status in the community? Or was she afraid, deep in her subconscious, that something unforseen and ghastly would occur to spoil it all, would turn this roseate dream into a nightmare?

A too-cheerful voice said, "Hi, there! Why the sour puss on such a fine day?"

Nora knew that the voice belonged to Penny Austin, one of her new friends of this glittering new world. She looked up, noticing that Penny's pale green blouse, complementing her fiery red hair, accentuated the swelling curve of her breasts. Her beautifully tailored linen slacks were delightfully filled by a well-rounded derrière above shapely thighs. Under her open-work Italian sandals her toe nails were painted precisely the shade of her flame- colored hair. She was, as Dave Osborne had once remarked, strictly a dish.

Nora forced a smile, said "Hi," and then, trying to overcome the chill feeling that came with the recognition of such formi-dable potential competition, she added, "Sit with me a minute, Penny. I guess I am feeling a little low."

"But why, darling?" Penny asked, seating herself in the near-est basket chair. She had come from the bar and Nora caught the aromatic fragrance of the tall drink in Penny's hand—her favorite, Nora knew—a doublerum planter's punch.

Glancing at her, Nora observed that Penny wore no lip-stick or make-up this afternoon and the heavy sprinkling of freckles against the creamy whiteness of her skin was exposed for all the world to see. The freckles and the pert, up-turned nose made her appear much younger her thirty-one years and Nora thought she could see what Penny had been like as a little girl.

But there was nothing of the little girl about the rest of Penny. Her lovely gray-green eyes were wise with the knowledge shared by all Eve's daughters and she was marvelously full-breasted and magnificently long- legged. No wonder, Nora reflected, that wherever Penny went, the males were sure to follow.

As did Dave, Penny's Bart worked for Worden-Forbes. He was head of Engineering and Design, which meant that he was a top executive. He had held that job for a half-dozen years and thus he and Penny had enjoyed their secure position in Lanford society for that length of time. Penny was a charter member of the gilded world that Nora had enjoyed only a few short months. Penny was at home in it. She had the self-confidence of experience, the savoir-faire born of belonging.

"What's the trouble, darling?" she asked. "Why should you be down in the mouth, for Pete's sake?"

"Maybe because I took my tenth golf lesson this afternoon," Nora said, "and I'm still a duffer."

Penny eyed her shrewdly. "You're not being truthful with Auntie. More than your golf game is bothering you, darling."

"You're right, of course," Nora said, reluctant to confide in the redhead. "A little something more but nothing important."

"Want me to guess what?"

"You couldn't, really," Nora said, laughing.

"Want to bet?" Penny retorted. Then she said soberly, "You're worried because the company—spelled with a capital C, of course—is keeping your Dave in a sweat over that vice-presidency. He's had all the grief and headache of the job for nearly six months but without the satisfaction of having the title. You're worried that somebody will beat Dave to that veep name plate and Dave will be dropped back to junior executive. Am I right or am I right?"

"Well, that is something to worry about," Nora admitted.

"You're thinking," Penny went on, "that Dave has proved he can play the game and you're trying to guess why he hasn't won the name, too. I'll bet your guess is that you yourself may be the stumbling block."

Nora squirmed in her chair, suddenly ill at ease. "Maybe it is that," she admitted. "Maybe subconsciously I might feel that Dave is being held back because somehow I don't measure up."

Penny took a swallow of her drink. "This stupid nonsense of a man's wife having to pass inspection before he can qualify for a top job," she said, sounding deeply disgusted, "is for the birds, really. It'll end up with bright young men asking the corporation's blessing before they propose to a girl. My God, what a thought!"

Nora laughed, but her voice sounded forced to her own ears. Actually, Penny's arrival had only served to increase Nora's depression. What if Dave's failure to get that vice-presidency were really her fault? A man's wife did have to pass inspection; that was common knowledge.

Penny went on, "Believe me, I was in the same stew before Bart got his present job. I was being sized up by the powers-that-be and their wives, and I just knew that I wasn't getting over with the wives. I've always realized that I'm pretty much on the tactless side and—"

"Oh, but that's not so," Nora said. "It's just because you have such an outgoing nature, Penny and ... well, you give something of yourself to everybody."

"Thanks for them kind words, honey," Penny said dryly, "but don't bandy them about. I have to ward off enough passes as it is without the whole world knowing that—quote—I give something of myself to everyone."

"Oh, I didn't mean—" Nora began, suddenly embarrassed.

Penny laughed delightedly. "You're a sweet kid, Nora Osborne, but you're a little on the naive side. Anyway, don't lose any sleep by blaming yourself, if Dave doesn't get his promotion. You're sure to pass inspection. Any girl as cute as you would. Sometimes I think that's all it takes—cuteness. My theory is that the wheels simply want to keep a stable of sweet young things for their own amusement."

"You don't really mean that, Penny?"

"Don't I? After all the passes I've had to cope with—passes made by Worden-Forbes' top brass?"

"You're joking."

"Me? A charter member of the Ninth Floor Club, joking?"

Nora looked at her in bewilderment. "What in the world is the Ninth Floor Club?"

"You haven't heard of the suite the company keeps on a permanent basis on the ninth floor of the Harrison Hotel?"

"No, I haven't."

"Well, how unenlightened can a person be?" Penny said. "You ask Dave about it." She took another, longer swallow of her drink. Then, with a trace of bitterness: "Anyway, my Bart didn't get to be Director of Engineering and Design through his own efforts alone. After all, there are plenty of other men as capable as Bart Austin—as the corporation wheels well know. And Penny did her share, believe me. She gave her little all to help her man."

Nora did not reply. She was sure that Penny could not mean what she semed to imply.

"Now I've shocked you," Penny said. 'Well, child, you'll learn. You've only been one of us for a few months. Give the gray-haired boys time." She stood up abruptly. "I've got to rush. I've been roped into helping with the new hospital fund drive and there's a meeting this afternoon. Oh, but it's fun being an executive's wife, Nora. Never a moment free from being a public-spirited, do- gooder."

She started away, then turned back.

After a moment of hesitation she said in a friendly, confiding tone, "About your Dave: He's all right. Smart, and a hard worker. But I have it from Bart that he isn't exactly aggressive enough. Tell him to be a little more pushy, darling. Tell him not to be scared of the brass. Do that, now—you hear?"

She hurried off, disappearing into the entrance of the bar.

Nora sat for a few minutes longer going over Penny's conversation and disturbed by her disclosures about the Ninth Floor Club. She told herself that she did not believe half of what the redhead had said. Penny had been pulling her leg. The top men at Worden-Forbes were not like that at all. She'd met most of them during the past few months, and without exception they seemed—well—quite proper. True, she had occasionally caught one or another of them appraising her in a speculative wolflike way. But all sorts of men gave her the eye, just as they did to any woman who was not downright repulsive. Men's minds were always on one thing—even Dave's. Many a time she had seen him look with warm admiration at another woman. At Penny, for one. Penny's lush figure always caught Dave's eye and he made no secret of it. But he did not mean a thing, really.

Still, what if Penny had not been kidding her? What if she, Nora Osborne, would have to cope with passes made by some man who could make or break Dave's career? Would she—could she—lend herself to such a thing even to help Dave?

She would not, she decided definitely. She simply could not. Such a thing as Penny had hinted at was unthinkable for Nora.

So Nora told herself but still she was troubled. She remembered bits of gossip she had heard, gossip about members of the crowd that now comprised Dave's and her friends. There was gossip of affairs and assignations. Perhaps there were deals made between the young wives of ambitious junior executives and the men who wielded the power at Worden-Forbes. Maybe there was more than one sort of payola.

Nora had come from a straightlaced, middle-class background and she could not shake off the sense of shocked dismay that such things actually went on among the people she now knew. Suddenly she did not want to think about it longer. She set down her unfinished Coke, rose and hurried to her Ford station wagon in the parking area alongside the clubhouse.

The station wagon was new and had replaced the ten- year-old second car she had formerly driven. Like the Buick that Dave had bought at the same time, the station wagon was a must. They had moved into a better neighborhood and so their cars, too, must have more prestige. Dave's income had jumped from seventy-five hundred a year to twelve thousand when he had been given the duties of a vice-president. On his own, he would not have moved from their old house in the inexpensive development until he had been given the title—and the permanency that went with it—as well as the duties of the office.

But he had been advised by his friend, John Fletcher, Worden-Forbes' comptroller, to make the change. John was backing Dave for the vice-presidency and he had urged the Osbornes to live on a scale consistent with that office. This, John had insisted, would permit them to socialize with the firm's top men and their families. Through socializing they would be accepted. And it was vitally important, John Fletcher had pointed out, that Nora as well as Dave be found acceptable.

All this meant, Nora reflected as she drove away from the Lanford Country Club, that she was constantly on exhibition. She must measure up to the concept, held by the corporation high brass and their wives, of a proper wife for a Worden-Forbes executive. She must prove to the company's elite that she was not only capable of giving Dave a happy home life but also that she was adept at functioning as his social partner. A rising young executive's wife must indeed be a helpmate.

But was a helpmate really expected to go as far as Penny Austin had intimated?

And was the answer yes, if the husband wasn't quite able to make it on his own?

Nora didn't know.

She wished she could stop thinking about it.

CHAPTER TWO

RIVING HOME along the curving, tree-shaded streets of Wilshire Heights, past the handsome ranch-type and split-level homes, Nora lost her uneasiness. Everything was snug and safe here and she was able to rid herself of the ugly, weedy idea that Penny Austin had planted in her mind.

The neighborhood was as substantial-looking as it was attractive, and the people who occupied these fine houses were, Nora assured herself, much the same as Dave and she. Most of them were, certainly, couples in love and faithful to each other. They were solid, decent families, who took loving pride in raising their children in these homes. The parents were church-goers; they belonged to the PTA as well as the country club. There was togetherness here and certainly morality. If there were misfits in Wilshire Heights, misfits like Penny Austin, they were in a very small minority.

Yes, Nora felt better now.

She turned in at her own house, a gray-stone and clapboard split-level on a full acre of landscaped grounds. Their home was still new enough to her to evoke a little thrill each time she turned into the driveway. Although far from being among the more imposing homes in the Heights, the house and grounds were completely beautiful in her eyes.

She pressed a button on the dash, and one door of the two-car garage rose magically. She ran the station wagon inside, pressed the button again, and the door descended. She switched off the motor, got out of the car and entered the house proper by a connecting door.

Mrs. Jensen, the housekeeper whom Nora did not really need but accepted for status' sake, was busy in the gleaming, appliance-loaded kitchen with early preparations for dinner.

"Any guests this evening, Mrs. Osborne?"

"Not tonight, Martha," Nora said. "Were there any phone calls?"

There had been none, Mrs. Jensen told her and she went upstairs to the bedroom she and Dave shared. The chamber was done in ivory-white provincial and it was, of course, her favorite room. Why should it not be, she thought. Here she experienced the intimacies of love with the only man she had ever wanted. Here in Dave's arms she was lifted by soaring passion to ultimate ecstasy. She was, for all her considering herself a rather ordinary young woman, an extremely passionate one. The pleasures of the flesh were for her an important part of being alive. She lived through many a day waiting impatiently for bedtime with her husband. When she heard or read of frigidity in women, she could not understand or even imagine such a thing. *

She removed the plain blouse, skirt and heavy shoes that she had worn for her golf lesson and then examined herself critically in the dressing-table mirror. There was nothing of the narcissist in her makeup. She did not admire her physical self.

She was of average height but she would have preferred being tall. She was curvaceous when she would have preferred being slender. Her features were, it seemed to her, too ordinary. But her hair, a rich, lacquer-like black, pleased her and her eyes, of gold-flecked brown, were certainly another good feature. When she was angry her eyes seemed to spark. When she was happy, as when in Dave's arms, they glowed. Or so Dave had told her on numerous occasions.

Removing her bra, for she intended to shower, she revealed shapely, roseate-tipped breasts. Too big, she thought with her usual self-disparagement but certainly, thank heaven, not quite so bovine as Penny Austin's. She—

The phone began to ring.

She made haste to answer, going to the extension on the nightstand between the twin beds before Mrs. Jensen had to bother to take the call.

"Nora Osborne speaking."

"Nora, this is Julia Hoyt."

"Oh, Mrs. Hoyt. How nice," Nora said, her mind conjuring up a picture of the caller. Though fortyish, Julia was as lovely and trim as a high-fashion model—a true honey-blonde with a patrician beauty. She was the wife of Brandon Hoyt, a Worden-Forbes senior vice-president and board member. "How are you?" Nora said, asking that trite question because she was a bit flustered. Julia had never before called her. Too, Nora stood somewhat in awe of her.

"I'm quite well, thank you," Julia said. "I called to ask if you and your husband are free this evening. Brandon and I are having an informal little party—a cookout, actually, with just a few friends in, and we'd like so much to have you come."

"Why, we'd love to come," Nora said, trying to keep sudden excitement out of her voice, "unless Dave has already made an evening engagement today." She could not help feeling thrilled. This was the first invitation the Osbornes had received from the Hoyts. "Shall I call him, then call you back?"

"Oh, that won't be necessary," Julia told her. "Just come if you can. And I do hope you can. 'Bye now, Nora."

Nora said goodbye, thinking: Now we're really in. To be invited to the Hoyts meant that Dave and she were being accepted by them. It meant—

She had to tell Dave the good news right away.

She dialed Worden-Forbes' number, asked for Mr. Osborne in Public Relations. She was given Dave's secretary who asked who was calling. Nora told her and a moment later Dave came on.

"Hi, honey," he said. "What's up?"

"Guess who just called me, darling!"

"The White House."

"Goof! It was Julia Hoyt."

"Oh. Well, I'd never have guessed in a thousand years. What's with Julia Hoyt?"

"She wants us over this evening for a party," Nora said, then waited for her husband to express pleasure or even an excitement to match her own. When there was no response, she asked, "Well isn't that something?"

"Uh-huh. It's an invitation that was due."

"Couldn't it be a good omen, for heaven's sake? After all, Brandon Hoyt is a member of the board. And now that he and Julia are accepting us socially—"

"It must mean, you think, that I'm definitely on my way to that vice-presidency," Dave cut in. "Honey, for Pete's sake, don't pin your hopes for that on an invitation to a cookout."

"Well, I still think it's a promising sign," Nora said, refusing to be deflated. Then, after a pause: "Dave, honey ..."

"Yeah?"

"Could you come home, maybe?"

"At three-thirty in the afternoon?"

"I'm lonely."

"A nice cold shower is a cure for that sort of loneliness, baby."

"Beast!"

"See you about five-thirty, sweetheart," Dave said and broke the connection.

❧ ❧ ❧

In his office at the Lanford plant of the Worden- Forbes Corporation, Dave Osborne lost his smile the instant he put down the phone. A scowl replaced it. The scowl had nothing to do with Nora, however. Dave seldom had reason to be displeased with his wife. Nora became unreasonable only infrequently and he was pretty well satisfied with her. Pretty well? He was damn well satisfied with her. Nora was a doll, fun to have around at any time and especially in bed. That she was fun in bed was important to Dave, for he was, he would have admitted with all modesty, a pretty warm guy. At thirty-six, he showed no signs of slowing down in the bed department.

For a moment he considered doing what Nora had suggested, knocking off for the rest of the afternoon and going home to her—to take care of her itch. The thought caused his scowl to ease a little.

But the temptation of playing hookey passed and the scowl, which had come at Nora's reminding him of Brandon Hoyt, deepened.

The invitation to spend the evening with the Hoyts was not the good omen Nora believed it to be. For just this afternoon Dave had heard, via the office grapevine, that Hoyt planned to sponsor a retired Air Force general for the vice-presidency that Dave had been working for. Evidently Hoyt felt that Worden-Forbes should follow the example of other corporations that now numbered high-ranking military men among their top personnel.

What under the sun a retired Air Force general would know about business management and industrial production, Dave could not imagine. Of course, Worden-Forbes did manufacture electronic devices and space vehicles on Air Force contracts.

The general might be able to help the firm in its dealing with the USAF top brass. Perhaps that was what Hoyt had in mind.

Dave leaned back in his chair and lit a cigarette, then, still scowling, gazed about his office, or rather, he sourly corrected himself, the office he was momentarily occupying. It was a large room, with brown wall-to-wall carpeting, relieved by several small but good Oriental throw rugs. The desk was a conservative mahogany, the chairs and sofa of mahogany and brown leather. In one corner stood a large terrestrial globe, in another a flag of the United States. Three walls were panelled in walnut to shoulder height and finished to the ceiling in opaque glass brick, and the fourth was a picture window of reflectionless glass. By turning in his chair, Dave had a panoramic view of the company's fine new research and development building, set amid the well-kept, velvet-green expanse of lawn. And the atmosphere in which he worked was, of course, air-conditioned.

A voice in his mind: Boy, you're going to miss all this.

He would, indeed, when, and if he was moved back to the cubicle he had formerly occupied. He had worked in this handsome office for nearly six months now, ever since its former occupant, J. P. Vinson, then vice-president for Public Relations, had resigned unexpectedly and taken three key men from the department with him.

It had been due to the loss of those four top executives in Public Relations that Dave had been moved into this office and given the duties of a vice-president. He had been the only man left with the experience and ability to head the department. And, if anyone asked him, he had done a good job. He had reorganized the working routine to function more efficiently and had hired some good, new people to work with him. He felt that he was doing a better job than J. P. Vinson had done to protect and enhance the company's good name, both in the eyes of the organizations with whom Worden-Forbes did business as well as with the general public. On the other hand, he had the empty, bitter feeling that his efforts were not appreciated or even noticed by the big boys upstairs. Yet he realized that his non-recognition must be blamed partly on himself. Why was it that he could sell Worden-Forbes to the public but was such a flop at selling himself to Worden-Forbes, the people who mattered most in his present world? He was painfully aware of the deep-rooted shyness that kept him from tooting his own horn, but he seemed unable to conquer, or even to combat, this lack of aggressiveness.

Yes, it would be hard, damn hard, to go back to his old job as a junior executive. And costly, too. He would have to take a big cut and suffer the necessary retrenchments his lower economic status would demand. How could Nora and he possibly be able to keep the house in Wilshire Heights? Why, running the place kept him broke even now, on his two hundred and fifty a week.

The intercom on his desk buzzed softly.

He flicked the switch, said, "Yes, Miss Marvin?"

"Mr. Harmon of the *Herald* is on the phone," his secretary said from her desk in the anteroom.

Dave said, "Okay," and reached for the phone. "How are you, Mike?" he asked. "Something I can do for you?"

He knew the newspaperman well. As financial and industrial editor on the *Lanford Herald*, Mike Harmon was a good contact for a public-relations man and especially for one in Dave's job.

"Just confirm a rumor for me, if you can," Harmon said.

"What rumor is that?"

"Rather a big one. I heard that General Lyle Wyman, USAF Retired, will become a Worden-Forbes vice-president. Anything to it?"

"That is a big one," Dave said. "This is the first I've heard about it. How about letting me call you back?"

"Okay. But don't hold out on me, boy."

"Do I ever?"

Harmon ignored that, saying, "General Wyman is still hot news, you know. The ex-glamor boy of the wild blue yonder. How soon can I expect your call? I've got a deadline on my neck."

"Half an hour. Okay?"

"Right," Harmon said and hung up.

Dave's scowl was back when he put down the phone. Obviously, the rumor had been purposely leaked. And almost certainly the leaking had been done by the fly-boy's sponsor, Brandon Hoyt. Oh, Nora, Dave thought, you and your high hopes just because of a little invitation. This would hit her hard. He pressed the switch on the intercom and told Miss Marvin to call John Fletcher's secretary and find out if Mr. Fletcher could see him immediately.

Mr. Fletcher could, Miss Marvin informed him a minute later, and he went upstairs to the comptroller's office.

As usual, John Fletcher's oversized desk was littered with papers to the point of chaos. This was not due to untidiness on the man's part but to the nature of his work. As comptroller, he was constantly checking and rechecking the company's financial affairs and consequently he spent his days working his way through a paper maze.

He was a thin, gray man of sixty-one or two and he looked every year of his age. He wore glasses, and still seemed not to see too well. He smoked a pipe, and never appeared to be ruffled. A soft-spoken, mild-mannered man, he was not at all typical of the Worden-Forbes breed of executives. Somehow, he had taken a liking to Dave Osborne. In turn, Dave Osborne was more relaxed with him than he was with any other of the company's executive officers.

Reaching for his pipe, Fletcher leaned back in his chair and said, "Sit down and tell me what's on your mind, Dave."

Seating himself, Dave said, "John, I just had a call from the *Herald*. Mike Harmon has heard a rumor that a retired Air Force general, Lyle Wyman, will join the company as vice-president. I heard the same rumor here at the plant this afternoon. Harmon wants the rumor confirmed or denied. I thought I'd ask your advice before calling him back."

Lighting his pipe, Fletcher said, "How did Harmon learn of it so quickly?"

"The so-called rumor was leaked, of course."

"I suppose so," Fletcher said. "Well, I heard of it only a few minutes ago, myself. Brandon Hoyt was in here trying to sell me on Wyman. The idea is his. He served under the general during World War Two, and it seems that Wyman, since his retirement, has been putting out feelers to industry. Wants to find himself a soft, big- payment job now that he's retired from the service, just like a lot of other former brass. I can't say that I blame him, but—well, I question the value of most military men to industry. Business just isn't their game. Still, Brandon is enthusiastic. He's going to do a lot of spadework and then bring the General's name up at the next board meeting."

"There's only one vice-presidency open, John."

"Unfortunately."

"I feel that between Wyman and myself—"

"I know," Fletcher said, "You're the better man for the office. I agree absolutely. And I'm going to bat for you. Like Brandon Hoyt, I also happen to be a member of the board."

"He'll give you a fight, and he's tough."

"Yes," Fletcher said. "That, I know."

"Well, I'll just have to sweat it out," Dave said. "There's nothing I can do personally. But what shall I tell Harmon for publication? I can issue a statement either confirming or denying that General Wyman is to join the company. Either way, the next board meeting could prove me wrong. The only way I'd not be going out on a limb would be to say that Worden-Forbes hasn't heard the rumor. If I go to Hoyt, he'll most likely want me to issue a statement to his and Wyman's advantage. If I go to H. M. Forbes, the chief, he'll tell me that I'm the public relations man and bounce me out of his office."

John Fletcher chuckled. "Well, so you are the public relations man, Dave. And if you're a good one, you won't go out on a limb on this thing—even though you are personally involved."

Dave smiled ruefully. "You're right, of course." He got to his feet. "I'll give Harmon a statement that says absolutely nothing."

"Such as?"

"Such as: David J. Osborne states that no agreement has been reached between Worden-Forbes and General Wyman and that no negotiations are underway at the moment."

"So," Fletcher said, smiling, "you've solved your problem."

Dave showed that rueful smile again. "I guess my real problem was that I wanted to hear that Hoyt wasn't planning to bring Wyman into the company, John."

"Yes. And I wish I could tell you exactly that."

"Well, thanks for your time."

"Any time at all, Dave," Fletcher said.

Brandon Hoyt was getting off the elevator when Dave came from John Fletcher's office. Seeing Dave, he waited for him to come along the corridor. In his early fifties, Hoyt could have posed for a man-of-distinction ad. Middle-age had put gray at his temples and stamped his handsome face with character. He was lean and fit. He was also sharp and shrewd. Only one man in Worden- Forbes' widespread organization wielded more power than Brandon Hoyt, and that was Mark Hammond, retired president and current chairman of the board, who one day would almost certainly be replaced by Hoyt.

Hoyt had charm as well as distinguished good looks, and he now turned it on for Dave. He smiled, placed a friendly hand on Dave's shoulder and asked him how he was feeling.

Then: "Mrs. Hoyt and I are having a few people over tonight, Dave, and we'd like you and Mrs. Osborne to drop around. Make it about six-thirty, if you have nothing better to do. My wife has probably called yours by now, but I thought I'd mention it to you."

Dave nodded. "I'm sure we'll be able to make it, Brandon."

"Good, good," Hoyt said. "It's high time we got together socially. By the way, I've been wanting to mention another matter. I've already discussed it with John Fletcher and a couple of others and I feel that you should be told, in your capacity as sort of an acting vice-president." He paused, letting the significance of those last half dozen words register. Then: "General Wyman, a good friend of mine who's just retired from the Air Force, is looking for a connection with a concern like Worden-Forbes and I personally feel that he would fit in here. I'd like your opinion on the subject, Dave."

Choosing his words carefully, trying to conceal his feelings, Dave said, "I've a lot of respect for your judgment, Brandon."

"Then you wouldn't be opposed to the General joining the team, eh, Dave?"

"Not knowing the General, I could hardly be opposed."

"Actually, I'm merely sampling opinion."

"Oh?"

"It's not definite yet. It will be for the board of directors to decide, of course."

"The *Herald* contacted me about it," Dave said. "I'll have to come up with a statement for Mike Harmon over there."

Hoyt frowned with spurious annoyance. "Those newspaper-men," he said. "It beats me how they get onto something you're trying to keep under wraps. What sort of statement are you giving him?"

Dave told him exactly what he'd told John Fletcher. Then he added, "If you'd like something more definite, I'll be glad to quote you."

"No, no," Hoyt said. "Your statement covers the matter as it now stands. Let it go like that for the time being, and everybody will be happy." He gripped Dave's arm. "See you this evening, Dave."

He moved briskly away, and Dave, staring after him, supposed that he should be grateful. Hoyt had given him fair warning. He was not slated for that vice-presidency if Brandon Hoyt could swing it his way.

Thanks, Dave thought bitterly. Thanks so much for nothing.

CHAPTER THREE

ARRIVING home at five-thirty, Dave was greeted by a silent house. No sound of activity came from the kitchen. Evidently Nora had let Mrs. Jensen go home early, since they were dining out. Nora failed to appear to welcome him, contrary to her usual custom. Nor did she answer when he called her name.

He went searching for her. She was not in the living room, nor anywhere upstairs. He went back to the first floor and found her in his study, sitting in his favorite leather chair and turning the pages of his latest copy of *Fortune.* She did not look up. Her expression as well as her silence told him she was in a mood.

He sighed resignedly. "All right," he said. "Just what did I do?"

The silence continued, except for the sound of magazine pages being flipped.

"I asked you—"

"It's not what you did, Dave Osborne," Nora said, looking up at last. She wore her angry face, eyes sparking and lips thinned down. It's what you didn't do."

"So what didn't I do?"

"You know very well what you didn't do," she said, getting to her feet and dropping the magazine into the chair. "You didn't come home when I needed you. For all you cared, I could have been deathly sick and—"

"Sick, hell—You just wanted to be laid."

"I *what?*"

"You heard me," Dave said, his temper slipping.

"I certainly did hear you," Nora said coldly. "And you needn't be so vulgar. You can find more proper ways to express yourself, you know."

"Excuse it, please," Dave told her. "But I'm an illiterate." He stared at her, having seen her lips quiver. "Damn it, you're kidding, aren't you?"

Nora began to laugh.

He grabbed at her. She tried to elude him but too late. He caught her by the arm, turned her about, slapped her across the backside, not gently.

"That'll teach you not to get kittenish," he said. "After all, a man expects his thirty-year-old wife to have a little more sense and dignity."

"Twenty-nine-and-a-half-year-old wife," Nora said, rubbing where he'd slapped her. "But you could have come home, darn it."

"I'm home now," he said, pulling her to him.

"There's no time now," Nora said. "We're to be at the Hoyts' at six-thirty. You just have time to shower and dress."

"Dress for a cookout?"

"Well, don't wear that business suit, for heaven's sake."

They left the study arm in arm, and went up to their bedroom. Nora was wearing a housecoat and merely had to change it for a dress. Dave began stripping down for his shower, going to the bathroom wearing only his T-shirt and shorts. He took along a fresh change of underwear. When he came back to the bedroom Nora was wearing her dress, a beige sheath, and was sitting at the dressing table doing her face. Getting a sports shirt from the dresser drawer, he wondered how he was to tell her about Brandon Hoyt's sponsoring General Wyman for the vice-presidency she so desperately wanted him to have.

Noticing that she was watching him in the mirror, he said, "I wanted to come home, honey, but I'm not exactly my own boss."

"Just so you wanted to come, darling," Nora told him. Then: "You were scowling a moment ago. Is something wrong?"

"No—No, not really," he said.

He got into slacks, put on socks and a pair of loafers. He kissed Nora on top of the head, then went downstairs to the kitchen and fixed a drink. He took a swallow and went back upstairs with the tumbler in his hand. He knew that he should tell Nora about General Wyman but he still did not know how to do it. It would be a blow, no matter how gently he broke the news.

Nora paused in putting on earrings, saying, "Don't tell me you needed a bracer just to visit the Hoyts."

"Well, I sometimes find Brandon Hoyt pretty hard to take," he said. "I'm not exactly in love with the guy."

"How about Mrs. Hoyt?"

"Too old for me."

"Just so I'm half as attractive when I'm forty."

"You will be," he said, meaning it. "Don't fret about that."

"Dave …"

"Yeah?"

"What is the Ninth Floor Club?"

He gazed at her blankly for a moment, then with curiosity. "Where'd you hear about that?"

"From Penny Austin," Nora said. "I saw her at the country club this afternoon after my golf lesson. We got to talking about how hard it was for a junior executive to make top executive and how a man's wife must stand inspection. Penny mentioned this mysterious Ninth Floor Club, without telling me what it is. She said I should ask you about it." Rising from the dressing-table stool, Nora faced him. "Come on, give, darling. After all, I'm a big girl now."

"There isn't any Ninth Floor Club. It's just a gag."

"Penny says she's a member."

"She did, eh?" Dave said. Then, after a pull at his drink. "Why did she say it?"

"She was telling me how she helped Bart get to be head of Engineering and Design," Nora said. "She said she'd given her little all' to help him. If she meant what I think she meant—well, you know."

"Don't let Penny Austin put ideas into your head, sweetheart," Dave said, grinning suddenly. "From what I hear, she's got the morals of an alley cat."

"You think she did help Bart in that—that way?"

"All I know is the gossip I hear. A long time ago somebody told me that she was Mark Hammond's part-time mistress."

"Mark Hammond? The chairman of the board?"

"No less."

"But he's—old."

"Sixty-one his last birthday."

Nora thought about Penny Austin and Mark Hammond. She looked as though she felt shocked. Then: "So what's the Ninth Floor Club? Explain the gag to me, Dave."

"Well, the company maintains a large suite on the ninth floor of the Harrison Hotel," Dave explained. It's for putting up visitors from the firm's other plants and its branch sales offices and for VIP's who come to Lanford to do business with the company. If these people request feminine company and are important enough to be given the full treatment, arrangements are made to send women up to the suite. Call-girls, of course. One of the guys in my department takes care of it."

"Don't tell me that Penny is a call girl."

"I won't. The girls I'm talking about are real pros."

"But what did Penny mean, saying she was a member of the Ninth Floor Club?"

Dave shrugged. "I can only guess. She probably had dates with Mark Hammond there. But don't ask me about Penny Austin. I'm not one of her boy-friends."

"Still, I've seen you ogling her more than once," Nora said, making a face at him. "Anyway, my curiosity is now satisfied—about the Ninth Floor Club, I mean. Now shall we call on the extremely wealthy and socially prominent Brandon Hoyts?"

"I guess we have no choice," Dave replied, grinning at her. Then: "You look wonderful, honey. I like the dress."

"You should by now," Nora told him. 'I've worn it often enough. But I'm glad you think I look wonderful. You look cute, too."

They went downstairs together and Dave disposed of his empty glass in the kitchen.

As they went to the garage he said, "It's too blamed quiet around here. I miss the kid."

"I do too," Nora told him. "But we'll be driving up to Camp Wee-ni-toka on Sunday to see her. And after all, Louise has been gone only ten days."

"That's a long time for a seven-year-old to be away from home. And she'll be away almost three weeks longer."

They got into the Buick, Dave starting the motor and pressing the button that controlled the garage door.

As he backed the car out, Nora said, "We can't keep our child tied to our apron strings. It's not done any more."

"But camp," he said. "I don't know that I approve."

"It'll make Louise self-reliant."

"Like you?"

"Well, aren't I self-reliant?"

"You are. And you didn't spend your summers at camp as a kid."

"I had very few advantages in my childhood, darling."

"But you survived."

"Full of complexes and frustrations."

Dave snorted. He was silent until they had turned from their driveway onto Elm Drive. Then: "Sunday, I think I'll withdraw *my* daughter from Camp Wee-ni- toka."

"Over my dead body," Nora said.

He grinned at her. "You and your body. Always flaunting it."

"As you expect me to," Nora said. Then, in a more serious tone: "Dave, Penny was trying to be kind and helpful this afternoon. She told me you should be a little more pushy. She said you shouldn't be scared of the brass."

"Oh, she did, did she?" Dave said, his voice barbed.

"She said that Bart told her you aren't exactly aggressive," Nora went on. "And you're not really, you know."

"Thanks, Thanks a heap. Next thing, you and Penny Austin will decide that I don't handle my job properly."

"That's not so, darling," Nora said. "Everyone knows you're doing a swell job of handling your department. But you aren't pushy enough. You don't mix with the top men." She looked at him anxiously. "Am I making you sore?"

"Not at all," he said flatly. "You're making me feel just dandy."

"I just want to be of help. A wife has got to help."

"Yeah. Like Penny Austin helped her husband."

"Now you are sore," Nora said contritely. "I'm sorry, darling."

Dave merely grunted.

They were silent the remainder of the way to the Hoyt's estate in the Crestwood section. Brandon and Julia Hoyt lived in a huge ranchhouse that looked like something out of the pages of *House Beautiful*. It stood atop its own rolling hill in snobbish aloofness and was reached by a long, curving drive-way. Around back were tennis courts, a putting range and a swimming pool. A dozen cars were already parked in front of the house when Dave and Nora arrived and one of them was the Austin's Lincoln convertible. Penny, alone, was just getting from the Lincoln. Seeing the Osbornes, she waved to them and then waited until they had parked and gotten from their Buick.

His feelings still ruffled, Dave eyed the redhead with sudden dislike. But his new distaste for her did not keep him from admiring her as a woman. She had the ripe, statuesque figure of a showgirl and, at times, the pixyish expression of a sex-kitten. There always seemed to be an excitement in her just below the surface and Dave, in male fashion, assumed that was due to the fact that passion, sudden and explosive, lay at a shallow depth within her.

Penny was an outgoing person; that was sure. In greeting Nora, she exclaimed, "Darling, you look wonderful," and then touched cheeks with her in that ludicrous pretense of two females kissing. The next instant she turned to Dave and gave him a warm, sensual smile. The instantaneous thought flashed through him that there was a promise—even, perhaps, an invitation—in her crinkled green eyes.

"And you have that handsome husband of yours along," she said. "How are you, Dave?"

"I'm fine," Dave said. "And you?"

"Just fine," Penny replied. "Except I'm in a mood because I have to come stag. My husband is off trying to settle some damn problem at the Dayton plant. Look—may I make my entrance with you two? I just loathe arriving alone."

"Of course you may," Nora said. "Come along."

And Dave said, "Sure. Three makes no crowd."

He walked behind them around the house to the terrace where the cookout was being held. His gaze was on Penny's shapely rear. She made sure that he notice her by walking with an exaggerated swaying of her hips.

Two dozen or more people were already gathered on the terrace between the house and the swimming pool. Dave spotted a half-dozen Worden-Forbes executives. He recognized other of the male guests as prominent business and professional men. The women were, for the most part, middle-aged like the men, but were as sleek and lovely as expensive clothes, cosmetics and hair stylists could make them.

Brandon Hoyt saw the newcomers and came striding across the velvety lawn toward them. He was delayed by one of a foursome; someone who evidently had a story to tell for Hoyt smiled and nodded and finally broke into laughter. His wife joined him, and host and hostess came on to meet Penny Austin and the Osbornes. They made a strikingly handsome couple, Brandon with his virile good looks and Julia with her fine-drawn and rather cool blonde beauty. After telling Dave and Nora how happy they were to see them, Julia turned to Penny: "My dear, it was so sweet of you to come, even though Bart is out of town."

"I long ago decided," Penny told her, "that if I waited for my man to take me places I'd be sitting home most of the time. The guy's as much married to his job as to me—and maybe more so. And I think"—this to Brandon Hoyt—"that I hate Worden-Forbes with all the venom of a jealous woman."

"With Bart pulling down thirty thousand a year?" Hoyt grinned. "I'll just bet you do. Well, come along, you people, and we'll have some drinks. This little affair is by way of celebration—yours truly's birthday. The day actually isn't until Sunday, but we're celebrating now because I have to be out of town for the weekend." He smiled that charming smile. "Now please don't ask which birthday the old man is celebrating. That's a touchy subject."

Penny said, "You didn't warn us, and so we haven't come bearing gifts. Still. . ." She moved close to Hoyt, kissed him on the cheek. "So there," she told him. "Many happy returns."

Everybody laughed.

Each of the Osbornes privately decided that the evening promised to be a pleasant one; a forecast that made Nora warmly happy but one that filled Dave with a feeling of bitterness. For one fact stood like a threatening black cloud before his eyes: Their host, charming and hospitable though he was, was doing his level best to keep Dave from the vice-presidency.

CHAPTER FOUR

D AVE DID not purposely set out to get stoned but he was in a low mood from thinking constantly of that vice-presidency slipping away from him. So by nine o'clock, having drunk far more than he had eaten, he discovered that he was a little looped but he felt no exhilaration from his drinks. Rather, he was filled with an oozy, alcoholic self-pity. He stood around morosely on the edge of the crowd, working on his drink and taking no part in the talk and laughter of the other guests.

After Nora rebuked him by saying, "Really, darling, you're not being exactly the life of the party," he fixed a rather vacuous smile on his lips so as not to appear downright antisocial.

Actually, he had plenty of company in his mildly looped condition if not in his low frame of mind. The Hoyt's bartender was a busy man, and more than a few of the guests—both men and women—were feeling their liquor as much as Dave. But they were high rather than glumly tight and consequently the party soon showed signs of turning into something of a brawl.

There was, for example, the matter of the floating key. A dozen or so guests had gathered by the pool and the noise they made caused the Osbornes and still others to join them.

A man's voice yelled, "Go on, Georgie! Don't chicken out!" And another voice, no soberer than the first, called, "Go to it, boy I You've got everything to gain and nothing but your life to lose!"

Georgie was George Mason, famed as a playboy and heir apparent to Lanford's largest trucking firm. He was standing alone at the end of the pool and apparently contemplating a dive into the water. He had removed his jacket, shirt and shoes. As more and more people called to him to take the plunge, he grinned and said, "All right, here goes nothing!"

Quickly removing his slacks, he dived into the water and with a great deal of splashing started swimming toward a small yellow disc which floated in the center of the pool. The yellow disc bobbed up and down on the now agitated water, and Dave saw that it was a paper picnic plate from the buffet table.

Turning to Herb Sundersen who stood beside him, Dave asked, "What gives?"

Sundersen nodded in the direction of a young woman who stood at the edge of the pool, watching the swimmer with a half-musing, half-mocking smile. She was Connie Barron, one of Worden-Forbes' largest stockholders and a granddaughter of one of the company's founders. She had been recently divorced from a major-league ball player who had turned out, so gossip said, not nearly so virile as she had hoped.

"Connie floated her apartment key out on that plate," Sundersen said, chuckling, with the implication that whoever retrieved it could make use of it tonight."

"And Mason was the only taker?" Dave said. "Connie must feel let down that there aren't more chumps playing the game."

"Too many wives present," Sundersen said.

Nora tugged at Dave's arm and whispered, "Does she really mean it, do you suppose?"

"My naïve little wife," Dave said, grinning at her.

Mason finally came within reach of the paper plate. But he was both a clumsy swimmer and too eager, and in grabbing the plate he tilted it and the key slipped off and sank to the bottom of the pool. A collective groan, mingled with hoots of derision, went up from the watchers. A moment later several people called to the swimmer to dive for the key, Mason did make several tries at finding it but then, winded and tired, he was forced to come out of the water.

A moment later a second paper plate was launched, this one by Jim Matthews, vice-president of production at Worden-Forbes, and this plate carried not a key but a hundred-dollar bill. A heavy-set man with a coarsely handsome face and iron-gray hair, Matthews was a grass widower. He grinned, announcing that this was a contest for the ladies.

The ladies were more competitive than the men had been, and four young women decided excitedly to try for the money. One of the four was disqualified because of her tipsiness and one was restrained by her husband. The other two, Connie Barron and Penny Austin, quickly stripped to panties and bra, to the noisy delight of most of the spectators. They took their places at the end of the pool, waiting for Matthews to give the signal. He was agitating the water with his hand in an attempt to float the plate out from the side of the pool.

Matthew finally called, "On your mark. Ready. Go."

The two young women dived into the water. The spectators chose sides, some shouting encouragement to Connie and others to Penny Austin.

Dave Osborne watched glumly, rooting for neither. But beside him, Nora yelled excitedly, "Come on, Penny—come on!" Dave glanced at her amusedly. This wasn't at all like Nora. But she had been caught up by the spirit of the crazy stunts, probably because she had had one or two daiquiris more than her quota during the evening. "Come on, Penny—come on!" Nora cried.

Penny Austin was the stronger swimmer and drew ahead of Connie Barron. However, when they got close to the plate with Penny slightly in the lead, the Barron girl grabbed Penny by the hair. Penny's reaction was swift and vicious. She whipped about and drove her elbow into Connie's neck and Connie, with a shriek of pain, let loose her hair. Penny laughed and swam on and the next instant reached the plate. She took hold of it gingerly with one hand and with the other plucked off the hundred-dollar bill. Her supporters cheered, Nora among them.

Laughing, Penny swam to the side of the pool and was helped from the water by Jim Matthews. Her wet panties and bra clung to her like a second skin and her magnificent body gleamed in the soft glow of the garden lights. Wet though she was, she flung her arms about Matthews and kissed him. He slapped her on the seat of her soaked panties.

It was quite a party, Nora Osborne decided, a good deal wilder than the parties that Dave and she had attended before. She was a little surprised by that, since the extremely proper Brandon Hoyts were the hosts.

After the horseplay at the pool Dave and Nora went to the bar for another round of drinks. She was drinking too much, she realized. She felt a little tipsy. This will be my last, she told herself. She also told herself that this one should be Dave's last, too. He was drinking far too much but surprisingly he did not seem to be enjoying himself and she couldn't understand that. He no longer seemed peeved with her for her having said that he was not aggressive enough in his dealing with the key men at the plant. But something was certainly bothering him. She would have to ask him what it was when they got home.

A little later, feeling a fine warm glow from the last daiquiri, she went into the house to powder her nose. Coming from the bathroom, she saw Brandon Hoyt about to turn into a room farther along the hallway. Seeing her he stopped, then, after a moment of hesitation, he came to her.

"Enjoying yourself, Mrs. Osborne?"

"Immensely, Mr. Hoyt."

"I'm Brandon to my friends," he said, smiling at her.

"And I'm Nora to mine," she said. Then, noticing that there was still a smudge of lipstick on his cheek where Penny Austin had kissed him, she giggled. "There's nothing sillier," she told him when he looked at her uncertainly, "than a man wearing lipstick."

"I didn't know that I was," he said, grinning. He took out his handkerchief, wiped at the smudge.

"Tell me," Nora said, knowing it was the daiquiris prompting her. "Tell me. … Doesn't Mrs. Hoyt object to other women kissing you?"

"Not when I'm celebrating a birthday," he said. Then, eyeing her in a speculative way: "As for myself, I'm not averse to accepting kisses as birthday presents."

"Be careful," Nora said, and again felt the impetus of the daiquiris. "I can take a hint."

"Can you?" Hoyt smiled. "Well, if you're in a gift-giving mood—"

She was tipsy indeed, for she would never have considered kissing him when sober. She slipped her arms about his neck to do it. It was a brief kiss but a kiss, nevertheless, and with it she was committed. She would show him that at least one of the Osbornes was not shy with Warden-Forbes' executives. She slipped her arms farther about his neck, and this brought her body in contact with his. She kissed him again, more lingeringly. He put his hands at her waist, held her tightly to him.

Afterward, drawing back, she said, "Now. Many happy returns."

"I couldn't have had a nicer present," he said, and now his way of looking at her was definitely calculating. "We'll have to get together sometime, you and I."

"On your next birthday."

"That's a long way off."

"A safe way off," Nora told him. "And right now I'd better get back to the party."

"Look," he said hastily. "I'll call you one day soon."

"Don't you dare," Nora said, and in spite of her tipsiness hurriedly left him.

Dave and she left at eleven o'clock, among the first to leave. It was time to go home, Nora knew. Dave was well on his way to becoming stoned, and she—well, she herself had had far too much to drink. Her behavior with Brandon Hoyt was proof of that. Whatever had possessed her, she did not know. One thing was certain—she had left herself wide open for a pass. He had said he would call her and, worriedly, she knew he would. She remembered the direct, intimate look he had given her when Dave and she said good night to him and Julia ... Yes, he would call her. She felt suddenly frightened, actually frightened.

To get her mind off him, she commented to Dave that it had been quite a party.

"A brawl," Dave said, his voice thick and his words slurred. "That's what it was, a brawl."

He sounded not only more than a little drunk but also in a foul humor. She did not try to talk with him again on the way home, and once they arrived there he went straight to bed and was instantly asleep.

Later, lying in her own bed and listening to his slow, heavy breathing, Nora felt an annoyance that was very close to anger. She wanted him tonight, right now, this minute. She needed urgently to be loved. She was wide awake and in a state of excitement. She lay there thinking of George Mason trying to get Connie Barron's key from that floating plate. She wondered if Connie had taken pity on George and let him come to her apartment, anyway.

She wondered if Jim Matthews had not expected more than a kiss from Penny Austin for that hundred-dollar bill. And if Penny, with Bart in Dayton, had not known that Jim expected more.

She thought of her ridiculous behavior with Brandon Hoyt, and his promise or threat to call her, and wondered if her morals, like Connie's and Penny's, were not becoming a little elastic. Was it a case of when in Rome doing as the Romans do?

At any rate, she wanted to be loved tonight.

Her loins ached for male caresses, and her mind was full of sexual fantasies.

And her husband lay deep in sleep in the other bed.

CHAPTER FIVE

A FTER WHAT seemed hours, Nora finally slept and then over-slept. Dave's bed was empty when she awoke and the clock on the night stand indicated the time was nine-twenty. Dave had gone to the office without having awakened her. She wondered uneasily if he were still peeved with her and then, getting from bed and finding that she had a pounding headache, she also wondered how he managed to get up at his usual time. He must be suffering a much worse hangover than she was, having drunk so much more.

The door chimes sounded just as she came from washing her face and running a comb through her hair. They contin-ued to sound with urgency, unanswered by Mrs. Jensen. Nora became aware tardily that this was Thursday, the housekeeper's day off, and so she put on slippers and robe and went to the front door.

Penny Austin stood there and she was her usual buoyant self. "Hi," Penny said. She was in skirt, blouse and low heels. She appeared as bright and fresh as the fine July morning. "Did I get you out bed, darling?"

"Two minutes earlier and you would have," Nora said, forc-ing a smile. "Come on in, Penny."

Penny came in, asking, "Hangover?"

"Sort of."

"Me too," the redhead said. "But I've just got to rise above it. She frowned thoughtfully. "I know it sounds corny, but have you tried a cup of. black coffee?"

"Not yet."

"Let me make a pot for you."

"All right," Nora said and went to the kitchen with her.

She sat at the table while her visitor put water and coffee into the coffee-maker, and wondered about this early-morning visit of Penny's. The redhead lived only three blocks away but they were not on such intimate terms that they ran back and forth to each other's home. Knowing about Penny's extra-marital activities, Nora wasn't sure that she wanted to be on such friendly terms with her. Still, she did like her. Suddenly she realized that she was glad Penny had stopped by.

Penny sat down and lit a cigarette while the coffee perked and said, "It was quite a party, wasn't it? And as usual, I had one drinkie too many and made a fool of myself."

"How did you find the nerve, Penny?"

"I was just feeling devilish, I guess," Penny said. And then, in a serious tone: 'i came over to buck you up, Nora. As soon as I saw that lousy thing in the paper, I decided that I ought to lend you my shoulder to cry on."

Nora looked at her blankly. "What lousy thing?" she said. "I'm sorry, Penny, but I'm pretty fuzzy-minded this morning. And I haven't seen the morning paper."

"And Dave didn't mention it?"

"Mention what?"

Penny frowned. "Now I've done it," she said contritely. "I would have to be the one to break the bad news to you. Still, maybe it's nothing to be taken seriously—since Dave didn't say anything. It's just an item in Mike Harmon's column in the financial section of the *Herald*— something about a rumor of some retired Air Force general becoming a Worden-Forbes vice-president."

Looking stunned, Nora cried, "Oh, no!"

"As I said, if Dave didn't mention it …"

"So that was why he was in such a foul mood last night," Nora said, more to herself than to Penny. "He was worried about this. He didn't mention it because he didn't want me upset."

"He should have known you'd hear of it," Penny said. "A thing like this is like a pregnancy—you just can't keep it a secret. I'm sorry, Nora. I truly am."

Nora nodded, believing that the redhead was sincere. Getting from her chair, she said, "I've got to see it for myself. Excuse me, Penny, while I look for the morning paper."

She found the Herald on Dave's desk in the study. She opened the paper to Mike Harmon's column. The item, at the very end of the column, read:

> Interesting, to say the least, is the rumor that General Lyle Wyman, USAF Retired, is to join Worden-Forbes Corporation as a vice-president. W-F executive David J. Osborne in a statement to this column would neither confirm nor deny the rumor. According to Mr. Osborne no agreement has been reached between his company and General Wyman and no negotiations are underway at the moment.

This had been a blow for Dave and she—heaven forgive her—had made him feel worse by saying those things about his not being aggressive enough. What good would aggressiveness be against such a deal as this? A retired Air Force general. Damn. Why couldn't the man be content with having had one career? Why did this General Wyman have to take a job away from a deserving young man like Dave?

Poor Dave, she thought, and she felt like crying for him.

She returned to the kitchen and said bitterly, "Oh, darn, Penny, why did this man have to bob up? After all, there's only one vice-presidency open. That's the one Dave should have."

"Somebody at Worden-Forbes bobbed him up," Penny replied. "And I've an idea who that somebody is."

"Who it is?"

"Brandon Hoyt. He was in the Army Air Force during World War Two. A major, I think. Anyway, I'd bet that he's the culprit." She rose, saying, "You'd better have that coffee now, for sure."

They sat at the table, sipping black coffee.

After a lengthy silence, Nora said, "Penny, could you help Dave?"

"I?" Penny said, looking at her with astonishment. "How in the world could I help him?"

"Well, you helped Bart. You told me yesterday that you did. And Dave said—" She broke off, suddenly embarrassed. "Sorry, I didn't mean to say that."

"Sorry for what? For discussing me with Dave?"

"Well, yes."

Penny laughed. "Don't be sorry about that. Everybody discusses me—because everybody knows about me. It's not something a girl can hide. Not an affair with a man like Mark Hammond."

"Couldn't you talk to Mr. Hammond on Dave's behalf?"

'I'm sorry, Nora, but my affair with him is pretty well over and done with," Penny said. "He isn't the man he was when I needed a favor of him. He's six years older now and that makes a big difference in a man his age. I seldom see him any more—and I mean seldom. Actually he comes to Lanford only for board meetings nowadays. He spends his time between Maine and Florida. I'm sorry, darling, but I don't see how I could help."

"I shouldn't have asked."

"Sure you should have. And I only wish I could have said yes. That damned Brandon Hoyt. One day he'll replace Mark as chairman of the board and that day I dread to see."

"He told me last night that he's going to call me."

"Brandon?"

Nora nodded.

"Well, in that case maybe you can do yourself some good." Penny gave her a knowing smile.

"Oh, I couldn't. I just couldn't."

"You've never had any man but Dave, have you?"

"No, never."

"Really? What a rare bird you are."

"Had you other men besides Bart—before Mark Hammond?"

"A dozen," Penny said matter-of-factly. "The first when I was fifteen. My father came home from the war with a lame leg and a nervous condition. He was in and out of the veterans' hospital all the time and my mother took a lover. Or rather she kept the lover she'd had while Dad was in the service. My father and I had never been close. He was preoccupied with sports every spare moment and forever going out with the boys. He hadn't much time for a daughter—or for a wife, for that matter. My mother and I weren't exactly buddy-buddy, but I understood her. Somehow I understood her need for a lover—young as I was.

"Anyway, this boy-friend of hers, Max, was a sweet guy and nice to me. He was always bringing me gifts, when he came to see Elaine—Mother. Bribes, I guess they were, to keep me from telling tales out of school. The older I got, the nicer he was to me. So one day in the summer when there was no school and Elaine was at work, he stopped by when I was alone. He said that he'd just happened to be in the neighborhood but of course he'd planned it. He came with a present. Not a bribe this time; it was an enticement."

"And he was the first man?" Nora asked as Penny paused.

Penny nodded. "He was on the fat and forty side but that didn't matter. I liked him. More important, I was wild to know what really went on between men and women. I didn't know from nothing but I met him halfway ... My mother married him after my father passed away but that was after I was grown and had left home. After Max, there was a boy. He wasn't any good at it; too young and clumsy. There were others before I married Bart."

Penny paused, seemed to think about it. Then: "With me, sex has never had anything to do with love. It seems a separate thing—an urge, an appetite, sometimes a hunger. Bart's my guy, and I'm fond of him. He's the only man I've ever known that I wanted to spend my life with. But where sex is concerned, well, a number of other men have been more fun."

Penny laughed suddenly. "Lord, but I'm being candid. What is it about you that makes me yak-yak about myself?"

Nora smiled faintly, feeling too low to be amused. "Maybe if I'd gotten off to the same sort of start as you," she said soberly, "I might be able to play the game like you do. But I can't imagine my giving myself to another man. Besides, I'd be terrified that Dave would find out. Aren't you afraid that Bart may find out you're playing around?"

"He knows about me," Penny said. "He knew from the start and he's always acted accordingly. He's never said a word but he keeps the score even. He probably would have done his own playing around even if I'd been as faithful as you. Like a lot of men, Bart's a chaser by nature. He—" The redhead suddenly burst into uncontrollable laughter. "Does Bart know about me and Mark Hammond? I'll say he does. Mark did a crazy thing a few months after Bart was promoted to his present job. One stormy Saturday night, I remember that Bart and I decided we'd stay home. We had a couple of drinks and played gin, then went to bed early.

"We were having a cozy time—nothing wildly exciting, just making love like two people used to each other. The phone rang. Bart answered because his mother was sick and he was worried about her. But it wasn't Dad Austin; Mark Hammond was on the phone.

"If you knew Mark well, you'd understand his pulling such a stunt. It didn't faze him at all that my husband answered. He simply said, 'Bart, I'd like to borrow Penny tonight. My chauffeur is on his way to pick her up.'"

Penny paused to finish her coffee and light another cigarette, then continued, "Bart was sore, of course. But he couldn't object, or he felt that he couldn't. He was still feeling insecure in his job. He owed it to Mark, and knew Mark could break him as easily as he'd made him. So I rolled out of the hay, put on a dress and shoes, slipped into a raincoat and tied a scarf about my head. By the time I was ready, Mark's chauffeur was pulling up in front of the house. I ran out into the rain and got into the car and spent the rest of the night in the company's ninth-floor suite at the Harrison." Penny laughed again, this time a bit ruefully, as though at a joke on herself. "That was one time when Bart definitely knew about me."

"And still you have a good marriage," Nora said, marveling.

"A lot of good marriages in our crowd have a dash of infidelity mixed in with them," Penny pointed out. "It would be a sorry world if a little extramural sex broke up all the marriages touched by it."

"But my Dave isn't at all like Bart," Nora protested. "He'd never let me get away with cheating on him."

Amused, Penny said, "Are you trying to convince me or yourself darling?"

"You, of course," Nora said, smiling. "Why should I need to convince myself of it? I know."

"But aren't you, right this moment, half-seriously considering a little cheating—if it could help get Dave that vice-presidency?"

"He wouldn't want the job if I had to sleep around to get it for him."

"You could be right, of course," Penny said thoughtfully. "But he really wouldn't have to know."

"There's no sense in even talking about it, when there's no Mark Hammond offering me a trade."

"But there is a Brandon Hoyt. Remember? You said he's going to call you."

"Oh, that," Nora said, trying to dismiss the possibility as meaningless.

Penny, however, refused to drop the subject. "When a man says he's going to call you," she said, "he means he has only one thing in mind—to have you for a playmate. Believe me, I—" She broke off abruptly, having glanced at the wall clock. "Good Lord, it's quarter past ten already. I've got to run or I'll miss my date with the hairdresser." Snubbing out her cigarette she got up from her chair and smoothed her skirt. "I'm sorry I can't help you, Nora. I truly am. And I do hope this Air-Force general thing turns out to be a false alarm. Don't get up. 'Bye now."

She rushed off, leaving Nora full of confused thoughts—thoughts she did not like. She certainly was not, as Penny had suggested, considering having an affair with Brandon Hoyt or with anyone else in order to help get that vice-presidency for Dave. Why, what Penny had done for Bart and had hinted that she herself could do for Dave was no less than a form of prostitution. It was unthinkable—for her, at least. What the Penny

Austins of this world could do so casually, the Nora Osbornes could not do under any circumstances.

She was too much in love with Dave even to dream of being involved with another man for any purpose. She—

The ringing of the telephone startled her out of her train of thought. Certain that Dave was calling, she rose hastily to answer. Of course he would call, she told herself, because he had let her sleep this morning and had left the house without having seen her at all.

So she snatched up the phone and exclaimed, "Dave, I'm so glad you called! I've been—"

The man's voice that cut in on her was not Dave's. Her caller said, "Sorry to disappoint you, Nora. This isn't Dave; it's Brandon Hoyt. Remember, I told you I'd call."

Nora knew it was ridiculous to be frightened. No possible harm could come to her over the telephone, she tried to assure herself. But she recalled Penny Austin's saying a man had only one thing in mind when he called a woman—to have her for a playmate. If that was Brandon Hoyt's purpose in calling her, she couldn't help but be frightened. Her shaky voice gave her away.

"Oh, Mr. Hoyt … How are you?"

"I'm fine, thanks," he said. "But I thought it was to be Brandon and Nora. Or have you decided we shouldn't be that friendly so soon?"

Reminding herself that she could not afford to appear uncordial toward him, she said, "I'm sorry—Brandon I slipped up."

"That's better, Nora," he said, laughing. Then: "You know, I was thinking of you a while ago and wondered if you'd have lunch with me."

"Today?" she said, alarm knifing through her. And then, as though an automatic safety control were touched off: "I'm so sorry, but I do have a luncheon engagement—one that I really can't break."

"Oh, what a shame—for me. I was looking forward to seeing you today."

"I am sorry, Brandon."

"Well, another time, maybe?"

"Yes," she said. "Another time."

They said goodbye and then Nora, putting down the phone, realized her mistake. She had failed to close the door against another invitation from him. Instead, she had left herself wide open. And could she plead another engagement the next time he called? She could, of course, but only at the risk of alienating him. And she could not afford to lose his friendship. What shall I do? she worried. How can I cope with him the next time?

She was still searching for an answer when the phone rang again. This time it was Dave and her heart leaped at the sound of his voice. She felt safe now; safe in his love and in the security of their marriage.

"Hi, honey," Dave said. "How are you feeling?"

"A little hung," she said. "And you?"

"The same, but I'll survive."

"You're not still sore with me?"

"Could I be, really?"

"I hope not," she told him. Then, in a more serious tone: "Dave, Penny Austin stopped by and told me about an item in Mike Harmon's column. Have you seen it?"

"I've seen it."

"Is there any truth in it?"

"I'm afraid there is, Nora."

"Oh, Dave!" she said, her heart aching for him. "I wish you'd told me. You were worried about it last night, and I was—well, I was nasty to you. Dave—"

"Yes, Nora?"

"Penny says that Brandon Hoyt must be the person behind it."

"He is, all right."

"Oh, dam him. I'd like to tell him a thing or two."

"A lot of good that would do," Dave said dispiritedly. "It's just one of those things that can't be helped. Well, I've got work to do, honey. Take care of your hangover."

Nora wanted to ask if there wasn't something Dave could do, but he said goodbye and broke the connection. There was not, she well realized, anything he could do. It would be unthinkable for him to go to Brandon Hoyt and try to make Hoyt understand that he, Dave Osborne, was far more capable of filling the vice-presidency, because of his experience, than any retired Air Force general. It would be a serious breach of office politics, to begin with. And such an approach would never change Brandon Hoyt's mind, for he was far from the type to permit himself to be influenced by a junior executive. Such a man would never be swayed by anyone, except perhaps—No, dam it, Nora told herself, I won't even consider such a thing.

When Dave came home that evening they made a point of not discussing the threat to their future. It was as though each felt that if they took no notice of General Lyle Wyman he might quietly go away, as a nightmare fades from memory by midmorning.

Saturday afternoon Carole Sundersen called Nora and invited the Osbornes to an informal little get-together that evening. If Nora and Dave could make it, fine. Carole and Herb Sundersen—he was chief engineer of Worden-Forbes—would love to have them. But in the event that they had something else planned, that would be all right, too. Nora said that Dave and she had nothing planned and they would be delighted to come.

It was, after all, a duty thing. Herb Sundersen was neither a company officer nor a member of the board, but as chief engineer he was a top executive and therefore a man Dave should cultivate. Despite the very real threat of General Wyman, Nora refused to give up all hope. She had to force herself to believe that Dave still had a good chance to have that vice-presidency.

The party turned out exactly as Carole had said the gathering would be, small and informal. There were less than two dozen guests and some of them, having other engagements, merely dropped in for a drink or two. Most were Worden-Forbes people.

Brandon and Julia Hoyt were present, as were Bart and Penny Austin. Penny's tall, lanky husband, a quiet type with dark-framed glasses and a preoccupied air, seemed an odd mate for the vivacious, oversexed Penny. At least he seemed so to Nora, now that she knew what sort of a person Penny Austin really was.

There was a buffet supper but, as usual, the food was held to be of secondary importance to the drinks. In spite of the continuously refilled cocktail glasses and highball tumblers, it was a sedate affair—at the start, at least—compared to the Hoyt's recent party. Conversation followed the conventional pattern, with the men discussing business, the administration in Washington, the international situation, juvenile delinquency, golf and sex. The women discussing clothes, children, recipes, servants, scandals, golf and sex. No flagrant flirtations took place; no couples sneaked away from the main group. Yes, this little party was, Nora told herself, quite different from the brawl at the Brandon Hoyts' home.

So the evening went until midnight when couples began saying goodnight and making their departure and Julia Hoyt suggested that Herb Sundersen show some of his home movies. By that time the only remaining guests were Dave and Nora

Osborne, Brandon and Julia Hoyt, Jim Matthews and a blonde young enough to be his daughter, and Bart and Penny Austin.

Nora could think of nothing more boring than being inflicted with someone's home movies. She gave Dave one of those wifely looks that said, "Let's go home—now." But when Dave and Nora got up and started to say that they must leave, big, blond Herb Sundersen grinned and told them not to be in such a rush.

"Don't worry—you may be in for a surprise," laughed Herb. "My kind of home movies carry a built-in, secret ingredient that makes them different from the usual run. You'll see."

The others joined in, urging Dave and Nora to stay.

And Julia Hoyt winked tipsily at Dave, saying, "You won't be sorry. Herb's movies are way, way out."

So Dave and Nora stayed, and Herb's so-called home movies proved to be way, way out indeed. He showed them in the darkened basement rumpus room and Nora was grateful for the darkness. She would not have liked the others to see the shock and then the embarrassed enjoyment that must have shown on her face. She would not have liked seeing the expressions of the other guests, either, at such a time. For Herb Sundersen's home movies were unalloyed, raw sex.

The film was in color with a background-music soundtrack, and the title, *Love Down on the Farm,* gave Nora a hint of what was to come. She was seated in a lounge chair and Dave was perched on the arm. Like the others, Dave and she had each brought a fresh drink to the rumpus room. Dave looked down at Nora, and in the glare from the screen she saw him grin. He, too, now knew what they were about to see and, like herself, he felt a bit shamefaced about it.

The first scene was of the house and barn on a typical small farm. A closer shot showed two men loading a pickup truck with sacks of grain. The one man was in late middle age, a homely sort, a true rustic type. The other was young, handsome. From their actions, apparently the older man was the owner of the farm and the younger one his hired hand.

The truck loaded, the farmhand disappeared into the barn. The farmer looked toward the house and a strikingly attractive blonde came from it and walked toward him. She was a most unlikely farm woman, for she had an unmistakable boudoir look even though she wore a simple house dress and an apron.

Obviously she wore nothing beneath the dress. Her over-sized breasts bounced freely and her heavy thighs were outlined with each seductive, hip-swaying step she took. She kissed the farmer and he embraced and fondled her. Clearly they were hus-band and wife. As he got into the truck and drove off she waved goodbye, smiling fondly. But once the truck was out of sight, she turned and hurriedly entered the barn. She began climbing the ladder to the hay loft, the camera remaining on her shapely legs as she climbed.

Comments came from the audience. Jim Matthews burst out, "So that's what farm life is like! Brother!"

Bert Austin said, "Boy, what a pair of gams!"

And when the girl on the screen reached the hay loft and found the young farmhand waiting there, Penny Austin exclaimed, "An honest-to-gosh roll in the hay!"

At that, Julia Hoyt asked, "Dave, Nora, now aren't you glad you stayed?"

Nora was at first amazed and then somehow disappointed in Julia, who had always seemed to her so proper, so much the lady.

The action on the screen had moved swiftly until this point. Now the film took on a more leisurely pace, showing the detailed, intimate love-play between the performers. They kissed and caressed and gradually the woman became the aggressor. She ripped off the man's shirt and flung it down, baring his heavy chest and torso. She ran her hands sensuously over his well-muscled body, her face registering pure lust. She was either doing a superb job of acting or true sexual passion consumed her. Suddenly, and with frantic haste, she bared her lover's body further and lavished caresses and long, lingering kisses upon it. After this amorous display continued for some minutes, she stood up and began to undress herself. Hastily she tore off the ridiculous apron, the absurd housedress, and kicked off her shoes.

And Jim Matthews burst out, "Man, get a load of those knockers!"

The young woman had a magnificent body. Her breasts were large, bell-shaped, her waist small, her hips more than adequate, her legs long and perfectly formed. She posed wantonly for her lover, fondled her own body; then he, by now stark naked, seized her roughly. Their bodies joined, the two fell together into the soft bed of hay. They writhed against each other for a time, then at last entered the ultimate embrace.

There was a fadeout at this point and the next scene showed the two, looking sexually sated, dressing and descending from the loft. Outside the barn, they parted. The man mounted a tractor to which a cultivator was attached and drove out into the fields. The woman returned to the house.

The final scene showed the husband returning in his empty truck. As he stopped and descended from the truck, his wife came from the house and ran to him. She kissed him hungrily, took his arm, tried to lead him to the house. He shook his head, gesturing to show that he had chores to do. She persisted, thrusting herself against him and squirming suggestively. Her face again registered lust. The farmer finally, reluctantly, gave in and they went to the house. The film ended with the closing of the door and the audience was left to imagine what took place inside.

The screen went blank, and Herb Sundersen shut off his projector.

"Is that all?" Julia Hoyt asked, sounding disappointed. "Haven't you more, Herb?"

"Well, I've one more new film," Herb said. "It's called 'Loves of a Salesman.' But there'll be a brief intermission while I change reels."

Dave rose from the arm of Nora's chair, saying, "To take another like that, I'll need a refill. How about you, honey?"

Nora hadn't touched her drink, and said so.

Dave went upstairs to the kitchen, and Jim Matthews and Brandon Hoyt, with his wife's glass as well as his own, followed. Herb turned on a lamp so that he could see to thread the new film into the projector. With the room lighted, Nora avoided looking at those who remained in the rumpus room. She gave her entire attention to her drink, too self-conscious to meet the gaze of the others. She could not talk and laugh about the film as they were doing and she wondered if she were something of a prude. Yet, she had to admit, she had enjoyed the movie. The images of those two naked people, the man as handsome as the woman was beautiful, remained vividly imprinted on her mental vision. Sexually aroused, she wanted only to experience, this very moment, the same actions that she had watched on the screen. She wished she were home with Dave.

Penny Austin crossed the room to her and asked, "How'd you like it, Nora?"

Forcing herself to look up, Nora said, "It was different, at least."

"Shocked you, I'll bet."

"Well, a little. I wasn't prepared for that sort of home movies."

Penny laughed, moved away. To Herb Sundersen she said, "I'm going for another drinkie, darling. Don't you dare start the next show until I get back."

"Don't be too long," he said, grinning at her.

Herb did start the second film before Penny got back from upstairs and before Dave returned. This film, fully as erotic as the first, had run several minutes before Dave resumed his perch on the arm of Nora's chair. A moment later Penny returned to the rumpus room, asking if she had missed anything. Suspicion nagged at Nora. She could not help but wonder why Dave and Penny had remained upstairs after Jim Matthews and Brandon Hoyt had come down again. She had a bleak vision of their embracing, kissing. She knew that Dave had long been attracted to the redheaded girl and she knew also what Penny's morals were like. But then Dave slipped his arm about her shoulders and in the semidarkness cupped her left breast with his hand. That small gesture, along with the torrid sexual activity on the screen, made her forget her suspicion that Dave might have been engaged in a little sexual byplay with Penny while upstairs.

But when the film was over and the lamps lighted, she saw evidence that her suspicions hadn't been groundless.

Hurt and angry, she said, "You should at least have thought to wipe her lipstick off your face."

Looking startled, Dave took out his handkerchief and sheepishly wiped at his face. He was unable to get rid of all the lipstick smear.

Nora got to her feet. "I've had more than enough of this," she said, speaking in a whisper so that only Dave could hear. She was angry but still she didn't want to create a scene. "Take me home, please."

The other guests were also talking of leaving and everyone went upstairs. There was the usual lingering at the door while goodnights were said. Jim Matthews insisted upon talking about the films with Herb Sundersen. Penny Austin stood talking with Julia Hoyt and the redhead noticeably avoided the gaze of Nora who was staring daggers at her. She would be wary of Penny's friendship from now on, Nora promised herself. When Bert Austin cornered Dave, trying to talk him into playing golf tomorrow, Nora found herself alone. Then Brandon Hoyt joined her.

In a whisper intended only for her, Hoyt said, "Monday, twelve-thirty, at the Lakeview Inn?"

She stared at him coldly, angry with him because she was angry with Dave. Could he actually think those films had made her ripe for an extramarital adventure? "I should think not," she said, and turned her back on him.

"I'll expect you," he said and turned away to join his wife.

Finally Dave and she got their goodnights said, told Herb and Carole that they'd had a marvelous time, and went out to their car. Dave had had too much to drink and he ran onto the lawn when pulling out from behind Jim Matthews' Thunderbird.

"Be careful, for heaven's sake," Nora said sharply. "Or maybe, seeing the condition you're in, I'd better drive."

"Are you saying I'm drunk?" he retorted, bristling.

"You're certainly not sober," she said, "which has been proved by the way you're acting. And have been acting."

He did not pretend ignorance of what she meant. "Listen: about Penny—"

"Yes, about Penny," she cut in, well aware that she was being pettish and unfair. After all, she had engaged in the same sort of thing at the Hoyts' party with Brandon Hoyt. But she couldn't help herself. "What about you and Penny?" she went on. "How far did you two go, anyway?"

"How far do you think we went?" Dave said disgustedly. "Do you think I laid her, right there in the lighted kitchen with other people walking in and out?"

"Those other people came downstairs before Herb started his second film."

"All right. So we were alone for a couple of minutes."

"So what happened?"

"Nothing that matters, damn it."

"It matters to me," Nora retorted. "And I want to know."

He swore under his breath and the car gave a sudden lurch as he swung back from too far to the left side of the road. He should not be driving, Nora thought—but she was afraid to suggest again that she should take the wheel. That, she knew, would really make him lose his temper. Luckily they had only a few blocks to go.

After a moment of sulky silence Dave said, "If you've got to know, she made a play for me. She gave me a buss on the cheek. You know what Penny's like; hell, everybody knows her."

"She gave you a buss on the cheek, did she? And what, may I ask, did you give her in return?"

"I kissed her back but I didn't mean a thing. I'd had a couple of drinks too many. And that damn film of Herb's didn't do me any good."

He ran through a stop sign, realized it afterward, and swore again.

After that, Nora decided to hold her tongue before they did have an accident. She managed to keep quiet until they reached home and Dave had run the Buick into the garage.

Entering the house, she asked, "Did you arrange an assignation with her?"

He stared at her. "I did not."

"Maybe you'd better."

He looked at her, scowling. "Now what do you mean by that?"

"I mean that you might get her out of your system if you once had her."

"Damn it; I don't want Penny Austin—and you know it," he said, striding into the kitchen. "I've got troubles enough without getting involved with any hot-pants dame like her." He opened the refrigerator, took out a tray of ice cubes. "For that matter, I've got enough on my mind without having you climbing all over me about something as meaningless as a kiss sneaked at a party. I'm losing out on the chance of a lifetime. I can see us having to give up this house and all that goes with it and that's plenty to worry about. So lay off me." He got a bottle of scotch from the cupboard. "Do you want a drink, too?"

"No, I don't want a drink, too," Nora said flatly. "And I don't think you need one, either. You can't drown your failure, remember."

"So now I'm a failure."

"That isn't what I said."

"It's what you mean, though," he said, going on with fixing his drink. "I'm not getting that vice-presidency because I'm not pushy enough. If I were more aggressive, I'd be getting it instead of that fly-boy friend of Brandon Hoyt's."

"If you think that, maybe it's true."

"All right, so it's true," he said and took a long pull at his drink. "Then I suppose I'm just not man enough to land a vice-presidency."

"To hold it, you mean," Nora said and wondered why she couldn't stop harassing him. "You already have it. You just aren't able to hold onto it."

"Thanks for pointing out my lack of ability."

"Nobody has said that you lack ability," Nora replied. "But what's the use of arguing about it—about anything? I'm going to bed."

"Go ahead," Dave told her. "Goodnight."

As she undressed, Nora realized that what had happened between Dave and Penny was not the only reason for her bitchy mood. She was upset by everything. The worry of Dave's not getting the vice-presidency. The fear of their having to give up this lovely house and a gracious way of life. And the secret shame she felt for having watched—yes, and for having enjoyed—Herb Sundersen's movies.

Abed in the darkened room, she was too keyed up to sleep. She felt torn apart, shattered, by this sudden contention between Dave and her. For one thing, she was haunted by the frightening prospect of losing their hard- won status of living in Wilshire Heights, of slipping from their place among the upper echelon of Worden-Forbes personnel, which only now was beginning to accept them. But on the other hand, she did not like the sort of people she and Dave were becoming. They had raised their standard of living, which was fine. Yet at the same time they had lowered their moral standards, which was not fine. These people, she thought. These people with their ultra-virtuous façade, but with no sense of decency or morality. Apartment keys and hundred-dollar bills up for grabs ... Erotic movies ... Sneaked kisses and cheap thrills ... Men winning promotion through their wives sleeping around ... Assignations arranged. And Brandon Hoyt, trying to arrange one with her. "Monday, twelve- thirty, the Lakeview Inn. I'll expect you," he had whispered. Okay, then. Let him be there and expect her. He was due for a big disappointment.

A sleeping pill, she thought. Or a tranquilizer.

She certainly needed something to put her to sleep.

But Dave came upstairs before she could get from bed and go to the bathroom for a pill. She lay still, hoping he would think she was asleep. He undressed in the dark, then came to her bed without having put on pajamas. Anger returned, stronger than before.

"I don't want you in here," she said flatly. "I won't have you in here tonight."

"Listen, honey." His voice was thick from the whiskey he had drunk and perhaps with soaring passion, too. "Damn it, I told you that stuff with Penny meant nothing. Forget it, can't you?"

"I just wish I could forget it."

"You're being utterly childish," he said, sitting on the edge of her bed and pulling the sheet down from her. "And you're no child, believe me."

"Sure, I know," she retorted. "I'm a woman. And after those filthy movies and that alley-cat of a Penny Austin you need a woman. Any woman. Well, just get over your itch some other way—damn it!"

She tried to pull the sheet back over her but he would not let her.

"I'm having you," he said angrily. "You're letting me have you. After all, you're my wife and—"

"Dave, I'm warning you!"

He ignored that, as she somehow knew he would. For the first time in their marriage, he was refusing to respect her wishes when she did not feel receptive toward his sexual demands. Also, for the first time in their marriage, he was making no effort to change her mood through the gentleness, the breathlessly intimate kisses, and the increasingly sensuous caresses that always before had brought them together to the ecstatic peak of passionate love.

Now his hands closed on her nightgown and ripped it off her, then reached hungrily for her breasts. She cried out and struck at him with her fists. She hit him several times with all her might but he seemed not to notice. She put her hands against his chest and tried to keep him from coming down upon her. This savage was not the gentle Dave she knew. This was a brutal stranger intent upon raping her. Her anger became wild fury and she fought him fiercely. But she couldn't stop him. He was too strong, far too strong. He spreadeagled her, dropped his weight upon her, invaded her so roughly that she cried out with pain. She lay helpless beneath him, telling herself over and over that she hated him.

Finally she sobbed, "All right. Use me. Use me—and pretend I'm Penny Austin!"

And to herself she said, I'll never forgive him ... Never!

CHAPTER SIX

S UNDAY, THEIR day to visit Louise at Camp Wee-ni- toka, was gray and wet. Waking to the rainy morning, Nora's spirits remained at low ebb. She got reluctantly from bed and went to shower her abused body. She dressed in a skirt, blouse and low heels, suitable clothes for the trip and was ready nearly two hours before Dave awoke. She knew that he wanted to get an early start but, filled with disgust for what had happened last night, she did not awaken him. She was still determined never to forgive him for his mistreatment of her.

She ate a little breakfast, then got the Sunday newspaper in from the doorstep and went through it with nothing she read really registering. She wandered about the house and at last heard Dave stirring upstairs. He was a long time in coming down, lingering in his shower, over shaving and dressing. Hating to face her, she knew. When he finally came to the kitchen where she was fixing breakfast for him, he looked badly hungover and extremely sheepish.

"Nothing to eat for me," he said. "My stomach's heaving. Just give me coffee."

In silence she poured a cup of coffee for him and then began putting away the breakfast things she didn't need.

Dave sat at the table and sipped the hot black coffee. He kept glancing at her, trying to measure the extent of her displeasure. She felt that he was pretending to feel worse than he actually did feel, to play upon her sympathy in the hope that in pitying him she would get over her anger. She simply hardened her heart, reminding herself of the brutal way in which he had forced her to submit to him last night. Raped by my own husband, she reflected bitterly—the kind of people we've become. She turned her back to hide threatened tears.

"Nora, listen," Dave began hesitantly. 'ı—I'm sorry about last night. You've got to overlook it. I'd had too many drinks and—"

"I don't want to talk about it," she cut in. 'ı don't want to talk with you about anything. I don't even want to be with you today, and I wouldn't go except that I want to see Louise. You can make it less unpleasant by keeping your excuses to yourself."

"All right," he said sulkily. "Whatever you say. Are you ready to leave?"

But the angry tattoo of her spiked heels was his only answer as she hurried to get purse, raincoat, and the things she was taking to her daughter.

The camp was only a seventy-mile drive from their house but because of the rain the trip took them nearly two hours, two endless hours of bitter silence. Dave attempted two or three times to break through her chill remoteness and, failing to get a response, he built up a wall of his own. His was a sulky silence and when sulking he always reminded Nora of a small boy denied some hoped-for treat. Today, however, he did not seem an engaging child, as he had sometimes when he was peeved, but rather a horrid monster of a small boy. Anyhow, she decided, he was in too foul a humor for her to try to salve his hurt. Let him sulk, she thought; the hell with him.

The visit with their daughter turned out to be far from rewarding. Seven-year-old Louise, too, was in a mood and Nora tried to blame Louise's dourness on the bleak day. Actually, as lovely as Camp Wee-ni-toka was with the fine grounds and attractive buildings and cabins, the place appeared gloomy in such weather. But Nora had to face the fact that the other girls, most of whom were gathered in the crafts building, seemed happy enough. Only Louise seemed depressed.

They found her sitting alone at a table with a book open before her, staring vacantly into space. So deep was she in her gloomy reverie that she did not notice her parents until they reached the corner where she sat in her loneliness.

"Hello, darling," Nora said, trying desperately to sound cheerful. "How's mother's girl?"

"I'm all right, I guess," Louise said, her wide gray eyes focusing on them. "You're late. I thought you weren't coming."

She spoke in a heavy, dispirited way, while all around them the other girls chattered and laughed gaily. They sat at the table with her, and Dave, discarding his sulkiness, tried to cheer her by talking in a forcedly amusing fashion. He was usually good with the child, able to make her happy when with her, but today she did not react. She remained grave, merely smiling politely. Nora thought: Something's bothering her; she's no happier than we are.

Nora could see little of herself in her daughter who had Dave's gray eyes and light brown hair. She was tall for her age and very thin. That, too, was inherited from Dave. Her temperament was also like that of her father, Nora suddenly realized—divining the reason for Louise's unhappiness. She knew that the child was slow to make friends, holding herself aloof. Like Dave, she was unable to mix with and impress herself upon others.

Unable to draw Louise out of her moodiness, Nora tried to get her to tell what caused her discontent with this charming camp. Nora was positive that she knew but she wanted Louise to admit it, to talk about it.

"I just don't like it here," the child said. "I don't like the other kids. I want to go home."

"But, darling, this is such a pleasant place. There's so much fun and things for you to do up here, and there's so little for you to do at home." She looked about the huge room, at the forty or more other girls. Not another child was alone. They were all in pairs or small groups. "The girls seem friendly, honey. Are you sure you've tried to be friendly with them?"

"Well. . . Louise stared at her shoes, her lips pouting.

"You see? It's you who isn't friendly."

"That's not so. They just won't bother with me."

"They would, if you bothered with them. You've got to mingle with them, join them in their games and in what they do. You've got to be—well, more pushy."

"Yeah, pushy," Dave muttered glowering. "You've got to be—pushy." He sounded bitter. "You must be aggressive."

Louise gazed up at him uncertainly. 'What's aggressive?"

"Ask your mother," Dave said. "She can tell you better than I can."

So it went, and the entire day was a horrible bust. Like all their days of late, Nora thought bleakly. She tried to make Louise understand that only by offering friendship could a person receive friendship. She talked for a long time and at last assured herself that she was getting her message across. At any rate, Louise promised to try to be friendly and she did not say again that she wanted to go home. After spending the afternoon with her, Dave and Nora talked to her counselor, Miss Le- land, who seemed understanding and sympathetic. Miss Leland said that she was aware Louise did not easily make friends, so she was making a special effort to get the child to associate more with the other girls of her age group. She promised to single out one or two girls to make friendly overtures to Louise and perhaps that would help her get over her shyness. They were not to worry about their daughter, Miss Leland told them.

But as they drove home through the rain, Nora did worry. And Dave burst out, "We should have brought her along. Damn it, the kid isn't happy there."

Nora broke her wall of silence long enough to take a stand against that. "We certainly should not have done any such thing," she said firmly. "Even if she is a little unhappy at the moment, the camp's good for her. She'll learn, somehow, that she must make an effort to win the attention of others."

"Sure," Dave said, turning sulky again. "She's got to learn to be pushy—aggressive. We can't have her growing up to be a Mr. Milquetoast, like her old man."

Nora chose not to reply.

They stopped for dinner at a roadside restaurant and arrived home shortly after eight o'clock. Though it was still early, neither one suggested going out or having someone in for the evening. Dave fixed a drink and sat down to watch television. Nora settled down with a best seller she had read halfway through, but as her thoughts wandered, the printed words became meaningless. Louises's discontent was one thing more for her to worry about. Maybe Dave was right; maybe they should have brought her home. It seemed that she didn't know what was the right thing to do any more. She was all fouled up. And so was everything else.

At nine o'clock she went upstairs and prepared for bed. While in the bathroom, she swallowed a sleeping pill. She debated a moment, took a second pill and went into the guest room where she opened the bed, then locked the door. There, she told herself, that will show him. She was not going to be raped tonight.

For a while, she thought the pills were not going to work. Her mind was racing, worrying about so many things, that she doubted if anything could slow it down. And abruptly she felt herself relax and grow drowsy.

She slept soundly, and overslept. It was nearly nine o'clock when she groggily unlocked the door and trudged into the bedroom—the bedroom that she and Dave had shared—to look at the clock on the night table between the twin beds. The master's bedroom for now, she thought bitterly. Well, the lord and master could have it all to himself for quite a while.

Dave was gone, of course. His empty bed was so badly rumpled that she knew he had had a bad night. She washed and dressed and the morning was as bright and cheerful as yesterday had been dark and dreary. Not that the state of the weather could change her feelings.

The phone rang. Mrs. Jensen was calling to explain why she had not come to work today.

"My daughter is sick," she said, "and I've got to take care of her and her three little ones. I'm sorry to let you down like this, Mrs. Osborne, but this is an emergency."

Nora told her that was all right, and not to worry. Putting down the phone, she thought that Mrs. Jensen's absence today was just as well. Nora would have a chance to get used to doing her own cooking and cleaning again, as she would have to do when she moved away from Wilshire Heights. She would not be able to afford help after Dave no longer had the vice-president's duties and salary.

She went downstairs to the kitchen where she sipped a glass of orange juice while the coffee perked. Even after two cups of coffee, she felt fuzzy-headed from the sleeping pills and decided that a walk about the garden might be good. Wandering about, she noticed that something had been nibbling at the rose bushes and she made a mental note to spray them later. She could do some weeding, too. Weeds were coming up through the cocoa bean hulls that their one-day-a-week gardener used for mulch. She spent an hour in the sun, hoping its warmth would lift her spirits. But it did not help and she felt like crying when she returned to the house. She did not want to move from here. She could not—just could not—give up the place.

The phone rang again, and this time Brandon Hoyt's now familiar voice said, "Good morning, Nora. How are you? Have you recovered from the effects of the Sundersens' party?"

"Yes, I have," she said, her voice sounding stiff and unnatural. "I'm fine."

"Good. And you can make it for twelve-thirty?"

She tensed. Her hand ached from gripping the telephone so tightly. "No, I can't make it. I'm sorry, but I just can't."

"Try," he said, his voice soft as a caress and somehow hypnotic. "Try, Nora."

"Well, all right," she said, her voice still sounding strange to her own ears. "But I'm afraid I'll end up disappointing you."

"I hope you won't," he told her. "Goodbye for now, Nora."

He broke the connection, and Nora quickly put down the phone as though it were an extension of his person and could do her harm. She stood in a trance, gripped by the unsettling thought that no real harm could come of her meeting him for lunch. Some good might come of it. She might be able to convince him that Dave should have that vice-presidency.

She glanced at the wall clock. Eleven-ten. She hadn't much time to dress and drive up to the Lakeview Inn at Crystal Lake. Still in a trancelike state but hurrying, she went upstairs. She entered the bathroom and started the water running into the tub. She would have to look her very best. She would have to make a good impression upon him.

Then, removing her clothes, she thought with something akin to despair: Heaven help me, I'm going to meet a man. And Penny Austin's phrase came to her: man who—who wants me for a playmate.

CHAPTER SEVEN

CRYSTAL LAKE was in the mountains, a thirty-five mile drive, and Lakeview Inn, a resort hotel, stood on a bluff at the lake's eastern end. Nora arrived late. The time by the clock on the station wagon's instrument board was twelve forty-five when she pulled into the Inn's parking area. She had driven slowly, even though she realized that she would be late. And now she sat for a moment in the car, not sure that she wanted to keep her date with Brandon Hoyt.

She knew what he wanted of her and he might have already made arrangements. A room for the afternoon here at the Inn. Cocktails and lunch, and then the room … No, she wouldn't do it. She simply couldn't go that far, even if he promised to back Dave for the vice-presidency.

So convinced, she got from the station wagon and climbed the three flights of stone steps leading to the hotel atop the bluff. She had been here a number of times for Sunday dinners with Dave. The place was pleasant with a magnificent view of the lake, the cottages dotting the shores and the forested slopes. But today, lost in troubled thought, Nora had no eye for the view.

She entered the lobby and thought that the desk clerk, who smiled and nodded, must sense that she was there for an assignation. That was foolish, of course. How could he imagine that? He did not know her.

She crossed the lobby and entered the dining room where most of the tables were occupied and told the hostess that she was joining a friend. A quick glance about the room showed her that Brandon was not there.

"I'll try the cocktail lounge, thank you," she told the hostess.

Brandon Hoyt was one of a half-dozen people sitting at the bar. He got from his stool at sight of her, smiling with pleasure.

"I'd about given you up," he said. "But the waiting has turned out to be worthwhile. You look wonderful, Nora."

She murmured, a little self-consciously, "Thank you, Brandon," and managed to smile for him. She knew that she looked less than wonderful. She was not beautiful and hardly glamorous but at least she did look her best. She was wearing for the first time her new gold cotton dress with a flared skirt, and it became her. Dave had not even seen it yet. "I'm sorry I'm late," she went on. "I had a bit of trouble making up my mind to come."

"Why, for pete's sake?"

"Well, this is all so new to me."

"I see," he said. "Well, maybe I can make it easy for you. A drink will help. Would you like to have it at the bar or in the dining room? I'm already one up on you, by the way."

She said she would prefer her drink in the dining room and then, when they were seated and the waitress came, she asked for a frozen daiquiri. Brandon had started with a martini at the bar and now ordered another.

Once she began sipping the daiquiri she felt relaxed and even managed to tell herself that it was going to be all right, that she could handle him. She would merely say no about the room upstairs.

"Feeling better now?" he asked, smiling directly at her.

For an older man, she thought that he was strikingly handsome. When he smiled, he had all the charm in the world. And certainly he was no ogre.

"Much better," she told him. "Of course, I'm scared to death that someone we know will see us."

"The chances of that are small," he said. "None of our crowd comes here. That's why I chose it. But look around if you want to, and reassure yourself."

"There's only one person here who knows me," Hoyt said, after Nora could see no one even remotely familiar. "That's Jim Matthews' ex-wife and she won't mention seeing me. She and I are old friends, so we're safe. By the way, I've arranged to be away from the office all afternoon."

Nora felt a quick thrust of alarm, but again she told herself that she could say no when the moment of decision arrived.

After they had finished their drinks, Hoyt summoned their waitress. "We'll have refills, please," he told her. "But we'll order lunch first."

She brought their drinks a moment later and shortly arrived with their food, a chef's salad for Nora and Hoyt's cold-cut platter. By then Nora was wondering how she could bring up the subject of the vice-presidency. She wished Hoyt would give her an opening.

He said, "How about you? Must you hurry back to town?"

"Well ... Not too soon."

"Good. I'd hoped you'd have time to go out on the lake. I've a friend who has a small boat I can use."

That seemed harmless enough, Nora decided. Apparently he had no intention of suggesting that they go to a room here at the Inn. He would not move that fast, she thought, reassured. He will wait until the second time to make a pass, but—surprise—there would be no second time.

As they had their coffee, Nora still sought a way to mention the vice-presidency, convinced now that Hoyt would not bring it up. At last, she decided to plunge in.

She said, "Brandon, there's something I want to discuss—seriously."

"Oh?"

"You'll probably think me out of order."

He shook his head. "Never you, Nora."

That gave her courage and she continued. She told him how much the vice-presidency meant to both Dave and her. She tried to make him see that Dave's experience made him the man best qualified for the office. He listened, an expression of sympathetic concern on his face.

"I agree that Dave can handle the job fairly well," he said. "But he doesn't impress me as having the all- around ability to be an executive officer of a firm as big as Worden-Forbes."

"He lacks only aggressiveness, Brandon."

"An absolutely essential quality in a key executive."

"He'd have more self-confidence—and therefore be more aggressive—if he got the job."

"You may be right, but I still have my doubts."

"Your friend, General Wyman, hasn't had Dave's experience."

"His contacts would more than offset that."

"Then your mind is made up?"

He did not reply at once but studied her in a speculative fashion. Finally he said, "Not so completely that it couldn't be changed. The general is a good friend, but I'm not exactly in love with him. We'll talk about it some more when we're out on the lake." He gave her one of his most charming smiles. "I'll give you the chance to change my mind. Fair enough?"

"Fair enough," Nora said, smiling back at him.

He stopped in the cocktail lounge, leaving her in the lobby and soon he reappeared with a Thermos bottle of martinis he had asked the barman to mix for him.

"We'll need refreshments out on the water," he said.

They descended the steps to the parking area and there he explained that the boat was at a cottage on the other side of the lake. He suggested that they go in their separate cars, he leading the way. His car was a blue Cadillac and she followed it in her station wagon, across the high bridge spanning the end of the lake. They drove along the north shore road, passing attractive cottages, and at last they turned in the driveway of an elaborate summer home built of stone, redwood and glass, and parked their cars alongside it. There was no other car about and no one seemed to be at home. The boat was tied up at a small pier.

"Well change into swim suits and really get some sun," Hoyt said. "Maybe swim a little."

"But I haven't a suit along."

"I'll get you one inside. Come along."

She held back, gripped by uneasiness. "Brandon, is this your cottage?"

He shook his head. "It belongs to a lawyer named Bob Newman. He's a bachelor who usually has a bevy of girls up here for weekends. So he keeps extra swim suits on hand for emergencies. We'll change and leave on the boat right away." He sensed her indecision and added pointedly, "You want the chance to convince me that I should back Dave for that job, don't you?"

Now she knew. He made it clear that his plans for her were made and that he would see them through unless she was willing to spoil everything for Dave and for herself, as well. She had played into his hands by mentioning the vice-presidency. She could still back out, of course, but—

He said, "Coming, Nora?"

"Yes. Yes, I'm coming."

With that she admitted to herself that she would go as far as he wanted her to go—even the whole way. She could not do otherwise with so much at stake. With Dave's whole future, her own future, in the balance.

"Yes," she said again in a choked-up voice. "I'm coming.

CHAPTER EIGHT

THE SWIM suit was two skimpy pieces of green material, a bikini.

In the bedroom where she had come to change, Nora felt rebellious for a moment. She would not go through with it. It was all so—so sordid. And shoddy. His wanting her to wear such a thing, his thinking he could have her. During that moment, she thought seriously of walking out on him. But it passed, for she remembered what he could do for her—for Dave. Slowly, feeling foolish and ashamed, she undressed and put on the two tiny pieces of cloth that were supposed to be a swim suit.

He called to her, asking if she were about ready.

She went out to the living room, feeling more naked than she ever had felt in all her life. He was in brief swim trunks, his exposed body deeply tanned and hard-muscled. He handed her a plastic swim cap, saying that she would need it if they decided to go into the water. He also held his thermos of martinis, a pack of cigarettes, a lighter, and a rolled beach towel.

"Nora, you're as lovely as I knew you would be," he said, his gaze moving slowly and intimately over her body.

"And I'm also as embarrassed as anyone could possibly be," she said. "I've never worn one of these things before."

"It becomes you."

"In an overexposed sort of way, perhaps."

"You've no reason to be self-conscious, believe me," he said. "Shall we be on our way?"

They went outside and down to the twenty-foot boat with its green canvas canopy amidships and twin outboard motors at the stern. He cast off the lines fore and aft, then started the motors. She seated herself beneath the canopy as he took the wheel and eased the boat out into the lake.

Other boats were out on the water, most of them sailing about the lake's east end. They headed west and soon passed through a narrow channel between the shore and an island. In the distance only two other boats were in sight on this part of the lake. Few cottages stood along the shore here and soon Nora saw none at all. After perhaps another mile they went through another narrow channel also formed by an island close to the shore. Beyond this second channel, the lake narrowed from about a mile across to about a hundred yards and this water they had all to themselves. The wooded slopes were steep here, rising directly from the water. There was no space for cottages in this wild and primitive spot.

Hoyt put in at a small island, dense with trees and brush. He cut the outboards, jumped ashore with a line, pulled the boat in, then tied the line to a tree trunk. The journey had taken only a few minutes but to Nora this quiet spot seemed as remote as another world.

Coming back aboard, Hoyt asked, "Like it?"

"It's lovely—but so lonely."

"The loneliness is what I like about it," he said, unscrewing the top of the thermos bottle. "Once in a while I like to go off alone."

"Alone?" Nora said.

He grinned. "Alone—with someone like you."

"And you often come here with someone like me?"

He shook his head. "Not often." He took two of the cups from the nest in the bottle's cap, poured martinis into them. Handing her one drink, he said, "Not often, and not for a long time."

She did not believe that. He was too much at home at the Inn, at the cottage, in this boat. His manner with her was too easy, too casual. He did this often and no doubt had done it recently. With whom, she wondered.

"To us," he said, raising his drink to her. "To us in our island paradise."

She drank with him, wondering what the martini on top of the two daiquiris would do to her. She took another sip, looking at him over the rim of the cup. He was an extremely handsome male, she had to admit. But could she give herself to him? She had always firmly believed that it would be impossible for her to give herself to any man but Dave. Now she did not know. She might panic at the last moment. Certainly she would not enjoy it. The martini along with the daiquiris was doing things to her. She felt lightheaded; her vision was a bit fuzzy.

"How about a swim?" Hoyt asked.

'Why not?" she said, glad of the opportunity to put off the moment of decision a while longer.

She donned the plastic cap, went aft with him, then lowered herself over the side. The water here was only up to her hips but a little distance off shore it was quite deep. They swam side by side for perhaps fifty yards, then Nora knowing her limitations as a swimmer, turned back. He came after her, taking her in his arms when they were midway to the boat. They went under together, then broke surface and treaded water. His arms remained about her, holding her body to his. He kissed her lightly and she laughed and slipped her arms about his neck. She returned the kiss. They went under again and their mouths were still locked together when they surfaced. They parted, gasping and laughing.

After they had gotten their breath back, Hoyt reached for her again. This time he ran his hands exploringly over her body and strangely she did not mind. It was almost as though he were fondling someone else, while Nora stood off to one side as an interested spectator.

Suddenly he said, his voice taut, "Let's go ashore."

They swam to shallow water and waded to the small beach. She removed the plastic cap and ran her fingers through her hair. He went aboard the boat for the martinis, cigarettes and beach towel, then led her through the brush and trees to a tiny clearing. He spread the beach towel and they seated themselves upon it. Filling the two plastic cups again, he handed her one.

"I really shouldn't," she protested. "I have a low tolerance for liquor."

"Just this one," he insisted.

She sipped just that one; then, with an almost total sense of unreality about herself and what was happening to her, she stretched out on the towel. He lay beside her, smiling faintly, his hand on her bare midriff. She felt herself shudder at the contact, but she told herself that the touch of his fingers was not so bad. Not wanting to look at him, she closed her eyes.

His hand caressed her for a time, then his fingers began working at the knot holding the strip of green cloth about her bosom. Soon the knot came untied, and he brushed aside the cloth, baring her breasts. He fondled them, caressing and kissing them repeatedly, while she kept her eyes closed, silently telling herself that this was happening to someone else. Aided by the drinks, she was almost able to convince herself of that.

After a time, he removed the lower part of the foolish bikini and bared all of her to his eyes, hands and lips. He began to stroke her thighs, and she, feeling suddenly tormented, began to squirm uncontrollably. She knew now. She was discovering that it was possible to enjoy the caresses of a man for whom she felt no real affection at all. This was pure lust, sex without any relationship to love, but it was no less enjoyable. She was fully aroused now.

"Brandon," she gasped, parting her thighs. "Please!"

He laughed softly, took his hands off her. She cried out with a shock, the pleasant shock, of his penetration. She wrapped her arms tightly about him and as of its own volition her body shared the rhythmic motion of his. He did not hurry. Indeed, it was a prolonged union. But it seemed all too short for her. She reached ecstatic fulfillment much too soon, and then, a moment later, he was experiencing the same tremendous explosive sensation. She held him even more tightly, wanting to enjoy with him every convulsive spasm.

Afterward, when his body was gone from hers, Nora lay there limply in an emotional calm, feeling physically spent and mentally inert. When she began to think, she marveled at herself. She had actually enjoyed it, which proved that she had not really known herself until this moment.

For a brief interval she was nagged by guilt. Then that, too, passed when she told herself that she had given her body to this man beside her for the best purpose in the world for any woman—to help her husband, to keep their home intact, and to assure their own and their daughter's future.

She recalled having read somewhere that after infidelity women were less bothered by their conscience than men. She now believed that to be true and was grateful for her own sake as well as that of all other women. She could return home to Dave and put this out of her mind. What had happened that afternoon was done and could not be undone, and she was sure that some good was bound to come of it.

If any part of the affair would continue to bother her, that would be the fact that she had enjoyed it so much. That troubled her even now. Uneasily, she wondered if she was by nature a—well, another Penny Austin.

The man who had been her lover, her extremely accomplished lover, raised himself on an elbow so that he could look down into her face.

"Another drink?" he asked. "A cigarette?"

"No, thanks. Nothing."

"Are you all right?"

"Very much all right."

"No regrets?"

"Not a one."

"Did I please you?"

"Yes. Oh, yes!"

He laughed softly, said, "We'll get along, you and I."

She looked up into his eyes. "Does that mean what I hope it does? That you'll back Dave for the vice-presidency?"

"As I told you," he replied, "I'm not exactly in love with General Lyle Wyman. Want to go back to the cottage?"

She said she did, because that seemed to be what he wanted. She rose to her knees and put on the no-longer ridiculous bikini. He gathered the things they had brought with them, and they returned to the boat. On the way across the lake she was both glad and sorry it was over. Glad because it should not have happened. And sorry because, like all stolen fruit, it had been so enjoyable.

When they tied up at the pier before the cottage, Nora noticed a small boat motionless in the middle of the lake. As she gazed toward it, there was a dazzling reflection of sunlight from some bright object held by one of the people in the craft. She wondered if someone were spying upon Brandon and her through binoculars and the lenses had caused the reflection. But that could hardly be, she assured herself, since no one had known she was coming here, and certainly Brandon would not have told anyone. Anyway, the boat now got underway and headed for the opposite shore. She promptly forgot it as Brandon patted her on the backside and told her to come along to the cottage.

Once inside, she went directly to the bedroom and removed the bikini. She had left the door open—privacy between them seemed unwarranted now—and Hoyt came in as she was hooking her bra after donning her panties.

"You're dressing?" he asked, sounding surprised.

She looked at him uncertainly. "Aren't you?"

"Well, I'd thought we could have each other again here," he said. "After all, it's still early—only three-thirty." He grinned at her. "Don't you want to do it again?"

She hadn't thought of it, but she said, "I want whatever you want. I want to please you, Brandon."

"Then come to bed with me."

Excitement instantly took hold of her. She slipped off the bra and removed her panties. They lay in each other's arms, facing each other, in no hurry this time. They kissed lingeringly.

After a time, Nora asked, "Tell me, why did you want me when you're married to such a beautiful woman?"

"Why, indeed?" he mused. "Well, I'm like a lot of men when they grow older. I have a yen for younger women. Even though Julia is a good wife, has given me a son and made my home life comfortable, it's not quite enough. You see, when I was a young man all my sexual experiences were with older—middle-aged—women. I was almost thirty before I bedded a woman my own age. I missed out on youth, so I crave it now."

"Why was that?" Nora asked, genuinely interested.

"I'd have to tell you the story of my life," he said, laughing. "And that would bore you."

"No, not at all. Tell me."

He moved away, sat up, reached for cigarettes. He lit two and handed one to her.

Then: "I was young during the depression. That doesn't mean much to you. Only people my age or older remember the really hard times. There could be no college for me and there was no decent job either. My father was an unemployed machinist. We were on relief. Rudy Vallee was singing about prosperity being just around the corner, but he didn't say which corner.

"I did any kind of work I could find. Odd jobs mostly and for what wouldn't even be tip money these days. I spent most of my time at the Y.M.C.A., at poolhalls, at the library. In winter, I was always glad when it snowed. The deeper, the better, because I'd take a shovel and go out looking for sidewalks to clean off—for a few cents. One night—a Saturday night, I remember—there was a heavy snowfall, but I didn't get many shoveling jobs. Too many men and kids were out for the work. I'd earned only thirty-five cents when I happened by the house of a teacher I'd had in high school.

"This Miss Anders was about forty-five, a stout and rather homely woman. She was shoveling her own walk, as most people did. I stopped, asked if she remembered me. She said she did. Flattered me to hell by saying she remembered me as the best-looking boy she'd ever had in any of her classes. For that, I helped her clean her walk. When we were finished, she asked if I'd like a cup of coffee and some cookies.

"I took her up on that—I was always a little hungry. She lived alone in a big old house that she'd inherited from her parents. Her home was pleasant, nicely furnished. The picture I got was that here was a well-off old maid. She had the house free and clear, I was sure. I knew her salary was about two thousand a year, which was big money in those days. While I sat in her warm kitchen, I began to get an idea—especially when she kept questioning me if I had a regular girl or went out at all with girls. I remembered reading at the library a biography of Benjamin Franklin. In it was some advice the old boy had given young men, advice about women. His idea was that older women could be very romantic— and very appreciative. From her interest in my nonexistent love-life, I thought that Miss Anders had an itch—possibly one she hadn't even admitted to herself. I decided to find out if she had. I thought—hoped—I might satisfy the itch if there was one and she might, in return, be appreciative to the tone of a few bucks."

As Hoyt paused to take a puff on his cigarette, Nora said, "And she turned out to have an itch?"

He nodded. "It was ten o'clock, which must have seemed late to her. But she invited me into the living room to listen to the radio. When the program was over she asked if I had to go home or if I could stay longer. I decided to force matters, so I looked her straight in the eye and told her there was nothing to keep me from staying all night if I wanted.

"She got the message—complete. And we didn't listen to any more radio. We were both virgins, but ... Well, we made out fine. The next morning the temperature was down to zero outside and we stayed in bed. We got up only to eat and to throw coal into the furnace. By evening I was worn to a frazzle but she begged me to stay. She'd give me ten dollars, she said. I stayed and in the morning when she got up to go to church I kept on sleeping. When she got home we spent the rest of the day as we'd spent Saturday.

"It ended up a regular thing, with my coming around three or four nights a week. And once a week she'd give me ten dollars. I really had it made. I gave some of the money at home, used the rest for clothes I badly needed. Then I heard about a job open at a third-rate movie house. I went around to see the man who owned the theater. He turned out to be a lush and the job turned out to be that of combination janitor and ticket taker. It paid seventeen a week. I took the job, even though I would have to work nights and give up my soft snap with Miss Anders."

"How did she take your quitting her?" Nora asked.

"Oh, I sold her to a pal of mine."

"Sold her?" Nora was aghast.

Hoyt chuckled. "For seven bucks. He was as hard up as I was and so I thought of fixing it up for him with the schoolmarm—for a price. He said he could dig up seven dollars, so I bought a bottle of cheap wine and took him around to see her. She was all broken up, didn't like the idea at all. But I opened the wine and in a little while she was happy again. It was a going-away party for me, a welcome party for him, and a change-of-pace party for her."

Nora thought about it for a little while, smiling amusedly. "Tell me," she said finally, "did you and your pal both have her that night?"

"Uh-huh."

"What a Casanova you were."

"Were?"

"Are," she corrected herself. Then: "Was there another older woman after your schoolmarm?"

"Another—and more," he said. "The movie house where I worked was really run by the owner's wife, since he was a drunk. She was a good-looking woman of about forty. And a smart one. She booked the films, checked out the cash every night, kept the books, made out the payroll, kept me and the other employees on our toes. Her husband spent most of his time in a nearby bar, but he always showed up—dead drunk more often than not—just before closing time. Sometimes he was so stoned that I would have to help her get him to their apartment. Even help her undress him.

"I got the same idea about her that I'd had about the school-teacher, figuring that a lush wasn't much good in the sex department. One night I made my pitch, knowing I would lose my job if I was wrong about her. We'd dumped him on the bed and she was pulling off his clothes, bending over him. I laid my hand on her derrière. She jumped about a foot, then swung around and stared at me. I just looked at her. Like Miss Anders, she got the message. After getting her husband settled for the night, she turned out the fight and we went into the hall. I started toward the living room, but she told me—sounding angry—to come with her.

"She led me into the other bedroom, took off her clothes, lay on the bed. 'All right, Hoyt,' she said. 'You asked for it. Now see if you know what to do with it.'

"After that I got twenty-five dollars instead of seventeen in my pay envelope each week. But that didn't last. After a couple of months the husband suddenly went on the wagon and I got fired."

"How sad," Nora said, laughing. "Did you find another middle-aged woman to pay your way after that?"

"That was when I wised up," Hoyt said. "By now I knew that old Ben Franklin's advice was sound and I figured that if older women were such soft touches, I might as well make working them my profession. Stud service, I guess you could call it. The idea I got then was to go where there were such women with real money. The answer was Florida—Palm Beach. So I hitch-hiked south. It paid off, even though my first job was that of bus boy in a restaurant. In time I became friendly with three well-to-do women, one a divorcee and the other two widows. One really set me up, gave me a start in fife. Every couple of months she would give me a certificate for a hundred shares of stock in a manufacturing firm in Pittsburgh. The stock was worth only a little more than a dollar a share at the time, but ten years later, I sold it at thirty-two. And I had seventeen hundred shares."

Hoyt smiled wryly. "Older women were my meat, back then, but now I need young stuff."

He took Nora's cigarette, dropped it and his own in an ashtray on the bedside table, then reached for her.

"We're wasting time, talking," he said, rolling her onto her back and forcing her thighs apart.

CHAPTER NINE

T HIS TIME, after they had finished, Hoyt immediately left her and went to the room where he had left his clothes. He returned fully dressed while she had only gotten into her slip. He lit a cigarette and gazed at her dispassionately and she sensed that he was impatient to get away from her. For her part, Nora felt drained and dispirited. Their love-making had been one time too many, she thought. They should have parted after returning from the island. Then the memory would have remained warm and pleasant.

Quickly she finished dressing, touched up her lips, ran her comb through her hair, then said, "All right, I'm ready to go."

They left the cottage, Hoyt making sure the door was locked behind him. Walking to their cars, they seemed as remote from each other as mere acquaintances, with nothing ever having been shared between them. To Nora came the unhappy feeling that she was but one of a long parade of women in his extramarital life. The thought depressed her.

Reaching his car and opening the door, he said, "Well, it was fun. I'll call you again soon."

She could not tell from his tone whether or not he meant that. At the moment she hoped he did not. How she would feel about it later, she could not guess.

"You'll keep your promise?" she asked. "You'll back Dave for the vice-presidency?"

"Of course," he said and got in behind the wheel "Don't worry about that."

He started the Cadillac's motor, put the car into motion. She went to her station wagon as he turned about in the driveway. He waved as he drove past, then he was gone.

She sat for a moment, unsure of him. Still, he had said he would keep his promise. He had told her not to worry. His abrupt departure meant nothing except that he had had enough of her— as she had of him—for the time being. Manlike, he would want her again and in wanting her again he would keep his promise. She would see to that. The next time he wanted to arrange an assignation, she would simply insist upon some assurance that he was dropping General Wyman and backing Dave. She would not give in to him again until she had that assurance.

She started the motor, turned the station wagon and drove away from the cottage. She saw nothing of the blue Cadillac when she reached the road. He was in a hurry to get back to town. She, too, should be hurrying for it was four-fifteen by the clock on the dash. She must get home and start making dinner before Dave got there; otherwise, he would question her about where she'd been.

But she did not hurry. Her mind was too filled with uneasy thoughts for her to drive at a high speed. She found that her conscience was going to bother her, after all, and she felt ashamed, guilty. And, too, she worried: What if I've played the role of whore for nothing? She had played it so well that certainly she should not be cheated out of her payment. The things she had done. She had wallowed in sex with Brandon that second time. She still had the feel of him in her nervous system. She had his male odor in her nostrils, his male taste in her mouth. She did not like herself very much at that moment.

By the time she was midway to town her spirits lifted some-what because of the remembrance that Penny Austin had won Bert his promotion by having an affair with Mark Hammond. Since Mark Hammond had kept his word to Penny, was there not a good chance that Brandon Hoyt would keep his word to her?

He's got to, she thought. He must!

At ten minutes past five she ran the station wagon into the garage. Dave would be home in another twenty minutes and she would have to make herself busy in the kitchen since Mrs. Jensen was not there to prepare dinner. Nora would have to appear busy—and innocent—so that Dave would not ask how her day had been and what she had been doing. Entering the house, she wished there were time for a bath. She had the foolish notion that Dave would be able to see that she was ... well, soiled. A leisurely bath would be the most wonderful thing in the world right now. She could wash away the taint of her infidelity, symbolically at least.

The phone began to ring as she entered the kitchen. She hur-ried to answer: "Hello?"

"Nora," came her husband's voice, "I won't be home until late. Same men from the Richmond plant are here and Bart Austin and I are elected to take them to dinner. It'll probably be pretty late."

She remembered last night and her sleeping in the guest room but knew that she could no longer punish him. After what she had done today, she could never again be peeved at any annoying thing Dave might do.

"It's all right," she said, no trace of a chill in her voice. "Mrs. Jensen isn't here, and I've not even begun to make dinner."

"You're not still sore?" he asked, sounding surprised.

"Of course not."

"No guest room tonight?"

"No, darling."

"Good," he said. "Well. I hope I won't be too late. I'll try to ditch these Richmond characters early. 'Bye now."

She put down the phone with a vast sense of relief. She had dreaded to face him so soon and now she had a reprieve; time enough, at least, to get herself in hand before he got home.

Upstairs she ran water into the tub, adding soap for a bubble bath and she remained soaking for a long half-hour, literally scrubbing herself pink. After toweling herself briskly, she put on lounging pajamas, combed her hair and carefully made up her face so that she would look attractive to Dave. She would love him tonight. Her mind was made up to that, tired though she was. Tired? She was half-dead. She could not understand why Brandon had exhausted her so much more than Dave usually did. Had she given more of herself?

She went downstairs and made coffee and a cheese- and ham-on-rye sandwich. After that skimpy dinner she went to the living room and sat down with the novel she had been reading for the past week, but read only a few pages when her eyes grew heavy. To keep awake, she put the book aside and turned on the television. She watched two programs, then lay on the sofa.

She would not sleep she told herself; she would just rest for a while. But she did sleep, and did not wake up until Dave got home and shook her by the shoulder.

"What time is it?" she asked drowsily.

"Nearly one, honey."

"One!"

"Things ended up with a lousy poker game," Dave said. "I lost thirty-two dollars, besides wasting the whole evening. Better come to bed, Nora."

She got up from the sofa, trying to stifle a yawn that would not be stifled. "Oh, dam; I did so want to be wide awake for you, Dave," she said.

She went upstairs, changed into a nightgown, opened her bed and got into it. Dave came up a moment later, after turning out the lights and locking up.

She said, "I was going to do it tonight, but now I don't think I can."

"Tomorrow night, honey."

"Yes. Kiss me now, before I doze off."

He bent over her, kissed her.

She was happy then, happy in spite of what had happened. Or maybe because of it. For now, she told herself, Dave was going to be named to that vice-presidency and everything would be all right.

They overslept in the morning and there was a frantic rush when they woke up and discovered how late it was. He had a nine o'clock appointment. He gulped the orange juice she had fixed for him but skipped the rest of the breakfast. He kissed her and left.

Despite not having him at all last evening and only briefly this morning, Nora felt surprisingly happy. She fixed breakfast for herself and ate more than she should have for her figure's sake. After eating, she put a stack of show-tune records on the hi-fi and then, with music to brighten her mood even more, she went upstairs to dress, make the beds, tidy up the bedroom and bathroom.

She spent a pleasant day, one uninterrupted either by the telephone or callers. She dusted and mopped the whole house, worked in the garden; then drove to the shopping center to buy steaks for dinner. She wrote a little letter to Louise, reminding the child to be a friendly person. She drove back to the shopping center to mail the letter, so that it would still go out today. Returning home, she bathed and dressed for Dave's arrival, still two hours off, wearing an outfit she herself did not care for but one she knew that Dave especially liked—a low- necked green blouse and a straight beige skirt.

She had made a mistake in buying the outfit really, for the blouse was too snug for her ample breasts and the skirt too tight for her very well rounded hips. Surveying herself in the full-length mirror on the bathroom door, she saw that the outfit revealed as much as it covered. Her breasts were separately outlined in two sizable mounds, while the shape of her buttocks was brazenly molded. She decided that she looked like a movie actress playing the part of a cheap floozie. But that was what Dave liked about this combination and she wanted to please him. Moreover, she wanted to feel that she was seducing him.

All day, even while busying herself, she had had sex on her mind. Though she had never been one to dwell unduly upon sexual thoughts when not engaged in the act itself, today she had had fantasies running through her thoughts in a constant procession. She had tried not to think of yesterday at the lake, but her imagination simply refused to co-operate. Because of yesterday, she was … well, in heat. She wanted desperately to make love, and she wondered, wryly amused, how she could possibly wait for bedtime, which seemed so far off.

The steaks were sizzling in the broiler and Nora was making a tossed salad when Dave arrived. His face brightened at the sight of her in the too-tight outfit.

"Well, well," he said, grinning. "Aren't you the sexy one?"

He came and kissed her, kissed her soundly.

"I've plans for tonight," she told him. "Martinis before dinner, whiskey sours afterward. No television. We sit in the garden until dark, getting slightly—just slightly looped. And then we go to bed."

"I'm afraid your plans are like those of the proverbial mice and men," Dave said. "John Fletcher is coming over this evening."

"Oh, no!"

"Oh, yes," Dave said glumly. "He said if we had no commitments for the evening he would stop by. I could not say no. After all, he's the one friend I've got among the top brass. I'm sorry, honey."

"It's all right," she said. "John never stays longer than eleven—and tonight I'll refuse to get sleepy."

She was a little disappointed, though. It would be a dull evening as was always the case when John Fletcher stopped by.

He would arrive promptly at eight, accept his first and only drink of the evening, discuss business from the comptroller's view point and then hint that he would enjoy a game of chess with Dave. They would go to Dave's study, and that would be it, for her, until John took his leave promptly at eleven. But he was a lonely man, a widower, and she could not really be annoyed with him for coming tonight.

The evening turned out as she had expected. Shortly before nine o'clock, Dave and their guest went to the study to start their chess game. She had been restless all evening and was more so now. She could not sit still to read or watch television. She could, she told herself, keep still for only one thing right now. And that would not happen until after eleven o'clock.

She got the idea of driving to the shopping center, both to be on the move and to pass some time. The stores closed at nine, except for the drugstore and she could certainly find an excuse to go there.

She looked in on the men at their chess game. "I've got to run over to the shopping center for some hair spray," she said. "I'll be back in half an hour or so."

Dave looked up, nodded and smiled as though he understood why she wanted to go.

The drugstore at the shopping center was next to the Pastime Bowling Lanes. As she got from her station wagon near it, a group of teen-aged youths standing in front of the bowling alley fell silent and turned their attention to her. One let go with a wolf whistle and another called, "Hello, Mrs. Osborne."

She glanced at them, wondering which one knew her and had called out but she could recognize none of them. However, she felt obligated to reply with a friendly hello. Walking toward the drugstore, she knew they still watched her. Kids, she thought—kids with grown-up ideas. She felt a little devilish and for their benefit she walked with an exaggerated movement of her hips. Again came the appreciative wolf whistle and she wore an amused smile when she entered the drugstore.

She drank a Coke at the fountain, then bought a can of hair spray that she didn't really need. She paused at the magazine rack, smiled at the pictures of bosomy females on the covers of the girlie publications. When she left the store, only one of the teen-agers remained in front of the bowling alley. She did not bother to undulate her hips for him.

Seated behind the wheel, she inserted the ignition key, turned it and stepped on the gas pedal. Nothing happened. After repeated attempts the car showed not a spark of life.

"Won't it start, Mrs. Osborne?"

She looked at the young man, a husky six-footer in a yellow knit T-shirt and dark slacks who was walking toward her station wagon. She found him vaguely familiar and frowned, puzzled, trying to identify him.

"The darned thing is completely dead," she said. Then, "I'm sorry, but I don't recall ever meeting you."

"We've never met, Mrs. Osborne," he said, his smile a flash of white teeth against deeply tanned skin. "But I've seen you around, often. Somebody told me who you are. I'm Phil Hoyt."

"Oh, yes."

She had seen him around and, of course, she had known that the Hoyts had a son. He seemed to resemble neither his father nor his mother so far as she could see. But he had a clean-cut, wholesome look. He was about seventeen, she guessed.

"Well, I'll have to call a garage," she said. "Do you know one that would make a service call at this time of night?"

"Why don't you let me drive you home in my car?" Phil Hoyt said, "and call a garage in the morning?"

"Well," she hesitated. "Maybe I should."

"Since the car won't start, you can leave your keys in it," he went on helpfully, "and the service man can fix it up, then deliver it to your home."

"A good idea, Phil, if you don't mind driving me home. I live over in Wilshire Heights."

"I don't mind," he smiled, opening the door for her. "Anyway, I'd like to show you my new car. It's a Corvette. Just got it last week."

She walked with him to his sports car, admired it enthusiastically, fitted herself into one of its bucket seats. He got behind the wheel, started the motor and switched on the headlights. They drove away from the brightly lighted shopping center but then turned off in the opposite direction from that which led to Wilshire Heights. She told him sharply that he was on the wrong road, but without answering her he pressed on the gas pedal. Puzzled and angered Nora watched the speed indicator climb from fifty to sixty, to seventy five.

"Listen, Phil, just what are you up to?" she demanded, frightened by him now.

"I want to talk to you, Mrs. Osborne."

"Talk to me? About what, for heaven's sake?"

"You should know, he said. "About your being up at Crystal Lake yesterday—with my old man."

CHAPTER TEN

STUNNED, NOHA could only stare at him. She would not have been more jolted if he had struck her suddenly and without cause. Long before she recovered from her shock, he swung the sports car off the highway onto a narrow side road running through a stretch of dense woods. After driving about a mile, he turned off onto a dirt road and the glare of the headlights showed orchards at one side and waist-high com on the other. Along the shoulders of this back road Phil Hoyt's headlights showed parked cars in which sat couples in prolonged embraces. Some of the cars were empty, their occupants gone into the deep shadows of the orchard or the corn field. A lover's lane, Nora thought dully.

She and Phil came to an old country schoolhouse, now long abandoned. Several cars were parked about the building, the radio of one tuned to soft music. Phil brought his Corvette to a stop at the deserted side of the schoolyard, as far as he could from the other cars. He switched off motor and lights and turned to Nora.

"Yesterday I was at Hutch's, a joint up the road from the Lakeview Inn," he said. "I saw my old man come down from the Inn with you, and watched you two drive to the other side of the lake." He grinned maliciously, white teeth gleaming. "My guess was that you were going to a cottage over there. So I hired an outboard at Hutch's also a pair of binoculars, then cruise out on the lake, looking for you love-birds. I saw you come back in a boat and go into a cottage."

Nora heard herself say, hoarsely, "I saw a boat, and a flash of reflected sunlight. I thought someone was watching … Did you do something to my car tonight?"

"Uh-huh," he said, grinning. "I took off the distributor cap."

"What do you want? My promise not to see your father again?"

"Not that, chick."

"What, then?"

"Don't be a square," he said, and cupped her right breast with his left hand. "I want some of what my old man had."

Nora felt suddenly sickened. "Phil, don't be ridiculous. I'm a married woman much older than you and—"

"So I've never had a married woman much older than myself. And that's what I want."

"You're only a boy."

"I'm as big as a man," he said, his hand squeezing her breast now. "Bigger than a lot of men."

She pushed his hand away. "I won't do it. It would be even worse than—than what happened between your father and me. Take me back and fix my car, please."

"You don't dig me, doll. The score is, you've got to put out for me. If you don't, I'll squeal. I'll tell my old lady about you and him, and she'll raise all kinds of hell."

"You wouldn't do such a thing," Nora said, uneasily and uncertainly. "Not to your father. Besides, you'd be hurting your mother as well as your father and me."

"So let everybody be hurt," he said. "I'll take you back, fix up your heap, then go home and tell tales."

She told herself he was bluffing. He had to be. It was not possible that even so precocious a boy would deliberately make trouble for his parents. "I won't do it," she said. "I just won't do such a thing. Now take me back to the shopping center."

He grinned nastily, seized her, pulled her against him. He pressed his mouth to hers, forced his tongue between her teeth. He slipped his hand under her skirt, grasped the soft flesh inside her thigh. She got her hands against his chest and shoved with all her might, thrusting him backward, away from her. The instant she was free, Nora opened the door and got quickly from the car. She thought frantically of flight but knew that was futile. Where could she run?

"Phil, please," she begged. "Please take me back!"

Still grinning, he got from the car. "Sure, chick," he said, reaching for her. "Just as soon as we've had our party."

She tried to elude him but he was quicker than she. He seized her by the left wrist, forced her arm up behind her. Then came a sudden, tearing pain in her shoulder and she had to clench her teeth to keep from screaming. Fearing that she would cry out, he clamped his right hand over her mouth. She was utterly helpless now. The slightest move on either her or his part caused her knife-sharp pain.

"Just do as I want, doll," he said, "and you won't get hurt." He applied pressure on her arm and the pain was so intense she feared she would faint. "Walk with me," he ordered. "Come on—move!"

She had no choice but to obey. He walked her toward a dark clump of trees, through it to a small clearing. He stopped there, his one hand still with its viselike grip on her left wrist and the other clamped over her mouth.

"You yell just once and I'll slug you," he said with low-voiced viciousness. "I'll slug you good. You catch?"

She jerked her head in a frightened, affirmative nod and he took his hand from her mouth.

"That's better," he said, when a moment passed without her attempting an outcry. "Why fight it, doll. Just relax and enjoy it."

He tried to force her to the ground but she said shakily, "Wait—Don't muss my clothes."

"You want to take them off?"

She nodded jerkily. She couldn't go home to Dave with any telltale signs of what had happened to her. He released her wrist at last but remained close, so as to grab her again if need be, while she removed her skirt and blouse. She laid them carefully on the ground, then he seized her and dragged her down. He tore off her panties, flung them aside, then roughly spreadeagled her. He came atop her, penetrated her with a hard thrust that caused her to gasp with pain.

She responded in no way at all, merely submitted to his frenzied use of her body. She was numbed physically, emotionally frozen. Her only reaction was shame and disgust. Fortunately it was quickly over. For all his size he was still a mere boy and did not know how to handle himself sexually. With no more than a dozen rapid thrusts, he came to completion. She waited, sick at heart, as he went through his series of climatic spasms and then, grown limp, removed himself from her. In a moment he got to his feet and zippered himself up.

Grinning, he said, "How was that, chick? The most, eh?"

"It was quick, at least," she said bitterly.

She picked herself up and hastily put on her clothes. She remained numb, frozen, from then on, only vaguely aware of their driving back to the shopping center, getting from his car into her station wagon. He raised the station wagon's hood, and after a minute or two told her to try the ignition. The motor started instantly. He slammed down the hood and she switched on the lights and drove away without another glance at him.

It was nearly eleven o'clock when she reached home. Dave and John Fletcher were at the front door, looking for her and worrying.

She stopped in the driveway, midway to the garage, and called to them in what she hoped was a natural-sounding voice. "I couldn't get the car started, dam it. I'd still be stuck at the shopping center if a kid hadn't come from the bowling alley and finally got it started for me."

"We were about to come looking for you," Dave said. "You'd better run out to the dealer's in the morning and have the car checked."

Later, after John Fletcher had gone and they were alone, she felt a little easier. Nothing about her showed, to Dave's eyes at least, what had happened. Dave and she had a drink and then went to bed. Locked in his arms, she tried to forget Phil Hoyt's fumbling use of her body. She tried, but did not quite succeed.

That morning, Thursday, Nora drifted into a low mood after Dave had left for the office. She had not been able to forget, even while making love with Dave, how Phil Hoyt had blackmailed her into submitting to him. And in remembering that, she was also reminded of her affair with Phil's father. She felt ashamed and guilty on both counts and she went about her household chores half-heartedly. Then increasingly upset, she called Worden- Forbes and asked for Mr. Hoyt. Hoyt's secretary asked who was calling.

"Mrs. David Osborne," Nora said reluctantly, yet knowing that any secretary of Brandon Hoyt's would be discreet.

Hoyt's voice, when he answered after a long moment, was brisk and noncommittal. "Hello, Mrs. Osborne. What can I do for you?"

"Have you a few minutes to talk, Mr. Hoyt?" she said, choosing her words carefully on the chance that the secretary was listening in. "I'm on the Hospital Fund drive and your name is on my list to contact. If you're busy at the moment, perhaps you would call back at your convenience."

"I'm afraid I'll have to call you back, Mrs. Osborne."

"Very well. You won't forget?"

"No, I won't forget," he said. "Goodbye."

He called back in twenty minutes, his tone now curt and unfriendly.

"You can talk now, Nora," he said "I'm at a phone booth. But, please never under any circumstances call me at the office. After all, I can't afford—"

Annoyed by his curtness, she cut in, "I didn't call because of a whim, believe me. Something very serious has happened. Your son saw us up at the lake."

Hoyt swore under his breath. "Has he been in touch with you?"

"He has, indeed," she said, and told him about last night.

She had expected him to be upset, and was shocked to hear him laugh.

"I'll be damned," he said. "Imagine the kid pulling such a stunt. I had him figured as too much of a mamma's boy for anything like that but I guess he's a chip off the old block after all."

"My God! You're not condoning what he did, for heaven's sake?"

"Well, there hasn't been any harm done, has there?"

"No harm done? How do you think I feel?"

"You didn't enjoy it?"

"Brandon, I don't understand you," Nora said, distraught. "A seventeen-year-old boy doing something like that. And there certainly was harm done, no matter what you think. Do you imagine I like being abused like that?"

"Abused?" He laughed. "That's a new word for it."

"I'm upset, whether you are or not. Why, he could try to make a steady thing of this—threatening to tell his mother if I don't give in. Can't you see that?"

"Oh, yes," Hoyt said casually. "He just might know a good thing when he has it. Well, if you really feel abused as you call it, and won't want it to happen again—"

"I don't, believe me!"

"All right. I'll have a talk with him. Don't worry—it'll be all right. Now I've got to get back to the office ... By the way, Nora, I'll try to arrange to take an afternoon off next week. I don't know what day it will be. I'll have to call you."

"I don't think you should bother."

"I thought we made a bargain on Monday."

"The only bargain I remember is that you promised to back Dave for that vice-presidency."

"But I understood that my promise on that gave me certain privileges."

"Well, perhaps. But first I want to be sure you intend to keep your word. I don't feel quite able to trust you, Brandon."

He laughed. "You've got to trust me, baby. Anyway, we're so good together that I should think you'd want a rematch. We were good together, weren't we?"

"Well ... yes."

"Anyway, I'll call you," he said. " 'Bye now."

He broke the connection and Nora stood holding the dead phone, her increasing uncertainty about him forming a cloud of worry in her mind. She could not trust him and she decided that her only hope lay in his wanting her again. Maybe if he wanted her badly enough, he would keep his word but that would mean a continued affair with him. And this morning, at any rate, she wanted anything in the world but that. She wanted to forget her one willing act of infidelity, and to become a faithful wife again. She wanted—

The door chimes sounded.

She put down the phone and, in her troubled frame of mind, started toward the front of the house. Penny Austin stood smiling in the open doorway—the last person she wanted to see this morning.

CHAPTER ELEVEN

Penny was wearing a sleeveless white blouse, brown shorts and green sandals, and she looked her usual delectable self. She smiled brightly. "Hi. Mind having a neighbor drop in this morning?" And she came in before Nora could answer.

Remembering the Sundersens' party and Dave with Penny's lipstick on his face, Nora felt a quick surge of anger. But then her reason took over and told her that she could no longer hold a few stolen kisses against Penny. Not after what she herself had done with Brandon Hoyt. The truth was, Nora told herself bleakly, that she and Penny were now sisters in infidelity. She was certainly in no position to cast stones at this lovely redhead.

"Coffee?" she asked.

"Uh-huh," Penny replied. "If you're not too busy. If you are, just kick me out."

"I'm not too busy, really," Nora said, pleasantly surprised to find that her rancor toward Penny had vanished.

But when they were seated at the kitchen table with coffee and cigarettes, Penny dealt her a low blow.

"What I really came for," the redhead said, grinning, "was to welcome you to the society of junior executives' wives who have given their all for dear old Worden- Forbes."

Nora stared at her, stricken. "What—what do you mean?"

"A little bird told me, darling. About your rendezvous with Brandon Hoyt at Crystal Lake."

Nora's heart sank; she was too jolted to speak.

Laughing, Penny went on, "Don't take it so hard, Nora. That sort of thing can't be kept a secret in a town the size of this. It's bound to be found out, sooner or later."

"Who told you, Penny?"

"Jim Matthews' ex, Karen Leighton."

Nora remembered Hoyt's saying that the woman was in the dining room of the Inn but she would not mention having seen them. He had been so very wrong. Or perhaps he had known and had not cared.

"But I don't know her," Nora said. "And she doesn't know me."

"She's seen you around and heard your name," Penny said. "But don't worry about it. Just because she told me doesn't mean she'll blab to anyone else. Karen knows the rules and plays the game. She told me because she knows I'm friendly with you. She thought I knew you were having an affair with Brandon. Dave won't hear of it. Husbands are never—but never—told." Penny took a swallow of coffee. Then: "By the way, how is he as a lover?"

"I—I don't want to talk about it."

"Oh, stop being such a prude, darling. It's too late for that. Besides, you haven't done what two out of three women we know don't do. So you went to bed with a man not your husband. So what?"

"I'm not exactly proud of it."

"Well, no. But you did it for a purpose and because of that you needn't feel guilty about it." Penny stared at her. "Are you such a prude that you didn't enjoy it?"

"I guess I did enjoy it, heaven help me."

"Sure you did—unless you're one of those unfortunate sexually frigid females. Did he promise to back Dave for that vice-presidency?"

"He promised but I don't quite trust him."

"I wouldn't trust him, either," Penny said. "I was luckier than you because Mark Hammond keeps his word. You'll have to keep working on Brandon, keep him panting for you."

"Even panting for me, he may not keep his promise."

"You should take out some insurance."

"Insurance?"

Penny nodded. "Get someone else to support Dave," she said. "Someone you can trust. Dave's got John Fletcher in his corner but John is a timid soul and won't be much help in a fight with Brandon Hoyt. Mark Hammond can be counted out. He's not here in town and I don't know if he'll arrive in time for you to work on him.

"At least three of the other board members can also be ruled out. Henry Forbes, our dear prexy, keeps a mistress in Baltimore and he doesn't cheat on her. Earl Holden is no chaser. Harlan Ames is an outsider, not connected with the company except as a board member and he does not live in Lanford. There's Vince Crane, though. He's an outsider but he does live here. He may be hard to meet socially, since he's not one of our crowd. Your best bet is Jim Matthews."

Nora stared at her incredulously. "You're not actually suggesting that I become involved with ¡him?"

"Why not?" Penny said. "You can't trust Brandon Hoyt but you could Jim—if he likes you. After all, darling, you're fighting for Dave's future. You've started to, anyway, and it would be foolish to stop at this stage of the game. Anyway, Jim Matthews isn't so bad. I admit he's a sort of roughneck but he's nice, in his heavy-handed way. And if he promises to back Dave, he'll do it. He'd give Brandon a fight, if Brandon continues to push his Air Force general. With John Fletcher, Jim Matthews and maybe Vince Crane on your side, Dave would be in—believe me."

Nora shook her head. "I couldn't do it. I can't see myself doing it again—and with another man. And I can't see how you can be like that, Penny."

"It's easy. I like that good stuff. The more, the better." Penny drank the last of her coffee. Then, eyeing Nora quizzically: "Honest, now wasn't it good? Didn't you have fun?"

"I don't like cheating on Dave, Penny."

"You were helping Dave."

"Well ... Yes."

"Keep that in mind. Quit worrying your pretty little head about being unfaithful. Anyway, you're still giving Dave his share, aren't you? You're not rationing him just because you gave in to Brandon, are you?"

"No, I'm not rationing Dave," Nora said. "But everything seems in such a mess." Suddenly she needed to confide everything in Penny who now seemed very much her friend. She told about her encounter with Phil Hoyt. "You see how fouled up everything is?"

"That kid," Penny said, laughing. "Imagine him pulling a stunt like that. How was it with him?"

"Not good."

"He needs more experience, a few years to season."

"Well, he can get his experience from someone else besides me. I've told Brandon about it, and he promised to talk to the boy."

"That was smart. Don't spread it around for free. If you must put out at this stage of the game, let it pay off. You give some thought to working on Jim Matthews and maybe Vince Crane too. That is, if you really don't trust Brandon."

Nora did not reply. But she couldn't see herself passing from man to man, from bed to bed, even to secure the vice-presidency for Dave. She was not like that. She was not entirely like Penny Austin.

❧   ❧   ❧

In his office at Worden-Forbes, Dave Osborne was giving some serious thought of his own as to ways and means of securing the vice-presidency for himself. He had an idea this morning, one that might give him a weapon to use against Brandon Hoyt. He considered it from various angles for a time, then had his secretary get Harvey Ward on the phone. Harvey Ward was in Purchasing, Brandon Hoyt's department. He and Dave were friends from high school days.

Into the phone Dave said, "Harv, it's been a long time since we've had a get-together. How about lunch today?"

"If you're buying, Dave-boy," Ward said. "The old budget is out of balance, and I'm not a credit-card man these days."

"I'm buying. Where do you want to eat?"

"You name it."

"Lorin's?"

"Fine, since it's on you. They make a swell deep-dish martini there and I haven't been in the place in months."

"Lorin's it is. What time do you go to lunch, Harv?"

"At twelve—always," Ward said. "Along with the rest of the working stiffs, since I'm one of them now. Or have you forgotten?" A trace of bitterness edged his voice.

"I haven't forgotten," Dave said. "See you at twelve, then." He hung up.

Dave lit a cigarette, sat lost in thought. What had happened to Harvey Ward was tough. He was now the lowliest of junior executives, hardly more than a clerk, actually. But until a year ago he'd been assistant to Brandon Hoyt and his future had looked bright. He had been given the job two years before when Hoyt's former assistant resigned to go with a trucking firm. Then, after the two years, Hoyt had brought in his nephew, a graduate of the

Harvard School of Business Administration, and had made him his assistant—putting Harvey back into his former job. Harvey had been given a raw deal but that, Dave told himself, was part of this game. A guy without pull had no security, and wasn't he the one to know that?

He had always hoped to find a way to help Harv and had planned, when and if the vice-presidency became his, to see that his friend was taken care of in some way. Now, because of the idea that he had latched onto, he was sure that Harv and he could help each other.

Ward came up to Dave's office a couple minutes after twelve o'clock. He was a thin, sandy-haired man whose heavy horn-rimmed glasses gave him an owlish look. Understandably, he was still bitter about losing out as Hoyt's assistant and habitually showed it.

Looking about Dave's imposing office, he said, "So this is how the upper one per cent have it. Think your title to that desk is clear, Dave?"

"Not too clear," Dave said, rising and coming forward. "You've heard the rumor about Brandon Hoyt wanting that Air Force general in this office, haven't you?"

"I've heard it. You letting him get away with it?"

"Not if I can help it. Let's go, eh?"

They drove to midtown in Dave's Buick. On the way, Dave inquired about Ward's wife, Lucy, and their two small sons. They were about as usual, Ward said glumly. Tim had a broken arm, and Dick an allergy. Lucy was unhappy because of his misfired career and the lack of money in the Ward household.

"Lucy still thinks I just failed to make good," he said. "And you know that wasn't the case, Dave."

"I know it," Dave said.

In the pleasant restaurant they were shown to a table immediately, had martinis and each ordered a medium- rare sirloin steak, baked potato, tossed salad, and coffee. When the waitress disappeared toward the kitchen, Ward picked up his drink.

"Here's to your tripping up Brandon Hoyt and that Air Force general, Dave."

After they had drunk to that, Dave said, "Harv, that's just what I want to talk to you about. I need help to trip up that pair."

Ward looked surprised. "Boy, if you think I can help you with that, you're just not well."

"I think you can help me—and help yourself at the same time. When and if I'm named to that vice-presidency, Harv, I'm going to take care of you."

"I've been hoping you would, Dave. It's about the only hope I've got left. But how can I help you, for Pete's sake?"

"Think back, Harv. Remember telling me, right after you got kicked out as Hoyt's assistant, that you had something on him and that you would use it except that you were scared it would backfire on you?"

"Oh, that?"

"What do you have on Hoyt, Harv?"

"He cut some corners while I was his assistant. Broke some company rules. One in particular."

"Which one? Give, man."

"Well, he was taking kickbacks from suppliers."

"I'll be damned. You're sure?"

"I'm sure. I was working with him, wasn't I? As head of Purchasing, he could work such a racket and get away with it. He had a thing going for him, believe me."

"And probably still does."

"He wouldn't give up a profitable sideline, that's for sure."

"Could you prove it on him, Harv?"

"I could. If I wanted to risk losing my job."

"How, Harv? What proof have you got?"

Ward looked uneasy. "Dave, I don't like this. I don't like it even a little bit. I can't gamble with my job, lousy as it is. I've my family to consider."

"You could be doing the right thing by your family. Just give me what proof you have and I'll have a talk with him. I'll cover for you and once I've got the vice-presidency, I'll bring you over into Public Relations. As soon as I can swing it, I'll make you my assistant. It could mean twice the salary you're now getting. Now give. What have you got?"

"A photostat," Ward said reluctantly. "A copy of a letter Hoyt wrote to the V. P. for sales of the Carmody Copper Corporation. In the letter, Hoyt said that he would procure a big Worden-Forbes order for Carmody, on condition that he received two hundred shares of Carmody common stock as a bonus for getting the order."

Excitement gripped Dave. "His signature was on the letter when you had the photostat made?"

"Sure."

"How'd you get hold of the letter?"

"I overheard him dictating it. After his secretary had typed it and he'd signed it, she placed it with the day's outgoing mail. This happened after I found out that I was to be washed up as his assistant. I thought I might use the letter as a club—but I lost my nerve. Anyway, I snitched it from the pile of outgoing letters on his secretary's desk. I took it home with me, the next day had the 'stat made, then put the original back in its envelope and mailed it. Nobody caught on."

"Harv, you've got to let me have the photostat."

"Dave, I'm scared to. Hoyt is nobody's fool. He'll know how you came by it. He could make the thing backfire on you—and on me. We could both end up out in the cold, cold world."

"We'll end up sitting pretty, believe me. We'll always be able to hold the photostat over him. He'll get down on his knees and beg me not to show it to anybody. Just the thought of H. M. Forbes seeing it would scare him witless."

Harvey Ward was a hard man to convince and Dave worked on him all the while they ate lunch. It was not until they were driving back to the plant that Ward gave in, and then he went along with the idea only conditionally.

"I'll have to talk it over with Lucy first," he said. "If she's willing for me to run the risk, I'll give you the damn thing. I won't take the chance on my own, then have her raising hell and tell me I'm a bigger chump than she thinks I am right now."

"You'll talk to her tonight?"

"Yes, tonight," Ward said.

Dave had to be satisfied with that. But he was tempted during the afternoon to call Lucy Ward and explain that his scheme would work. Before he had made up his mind to take that step, however he had a call from an acquaintance named Bill Marsten. The call made him forget Ward's photostat for the time being for Marsten, who had approached him before, had a job opening for him.

Marsten was head of Triton Electronics, a small but rapidly growing firm in a new and booming industry. He said, "Dave, I've been hoping since the last time I saw you that you'd get in touch with me."

"I've been pretty busy, Bill."

"Too busy to let me buy you a drink later today?"

"No, not that busy," Dave said, realizing that here was a chance to cushion his fall if he failed to win the vice-presidency. "Where shall I meet you, Bill?"

"How about the cocktail lounge at the St. Regis—about five-fifteen?"

"Right. See you then."

Dave put down the phone, asked Miss Marvin over the inter-com to place a call to his home. He would have to tell Nora that he would be late again. He smiled fondly, remembering how she had told him he was not aggressive enough. She would have to change her tune, once she knew what he was up to with Harvey Ward.

When he talked to Nora, he said, "I'll be an hour late this eve-ning, honey. I've an appointment to have a drink with Bill Marsten. You remember my talking about Bill some months ago?"

"The man who wants you to come work for him?" Nora didn't sound pleased. "Is he after you again?"

"Uh-huh."

"I'm not sure I like that, Dave."

"Well, the way things stand at the moment there's no harm in hearing what he has to offer."

"Don't commit yourself to anything, Dave—please."

"I won't. But it'll be reassuring to keep Bill's offer as a hole card—just in case."

"You're not going to need a hole card, darling. You're going to get that vice-presidency."

"Your woman's intuition tells you so, eh?"

"Well, yes."

"Do I detect a bit of uncertainty, though?"

"No, you don't. I refuse to believe anything but that you're going to get that job."

"All right, honey," he said, laughing, and put down the phone. Nora didn't want him to leave Worden- Forbes. She was counting on him to find a way to stay in this handsome office. Well, he was positive that he had found a way—if Harvey Ward would just play along with him.

He cleared his desk at a quarter to five and told Miss Marvin that he was leaving early. Walking along the corridor to the executive washroom, he noticed that someone was standing just inside the door, holding it slightly ajar, and talking loudly to someone farther back inside the room. He recognized Jim Matthews' booming voice and when he heard his name mentioned, Dave stopped several feet from the door, evesdropping on Matthews' end of the conversation.

Now he heard Matthews say, "Sure, it's true, Herb. I got it from my ex-wife. The cute little bitch keeps me posted—she should, the alimony she's getting. Anyhow, Karen says—"

Herb Sundersen, apparently, was the other man in the washroom.

"—that Dave has loaned that well-stacked wife of his to Brandon Hoyt. She saw them up at the Lakeview Inn together on Monday. You know what Dave's pitch is, don't you? He wants Hoyt to back him instead of General Wyman for that vice president's spot."

Dave felt as though he had been slugged. His brain reeling, he turned and walked back along the corridor, left the building and walked blindly to his car. For minutes, he sat slumped behind the wheel, telling himself that what he had heard was not true, could not be true. Matthews' ex-wife had simply been spreading lying gossip. But Dave could not convince himself.

Nora had openly told him that he was not man enough to win the vice-presidency on his own. She had heard about Penny Austin's winning Bart his promotion by having an affair with Mark Hammond. Nora had probably heard of other Worden-Forbes wives helping their husbands' careers by putting out. Hoyt must have made a play for her, either at the party he and his wife had given or at the Sundersens', and she had taken him up on it.

Nora—unfaithful!

My God, he thought—He wanted to bawl like a kid.

CHAPTER TWELVE

D AVE REMAINED in a state of shock and Bill Marsten, burdened though he was with the worries of a fast-growing company, asked immediately if Dave were not feeling well.

He could only reply that he was feeling a bit under the weather. "A lot of pressure on me these days, Bill."

"Better have a checkup. It could be more than pressure."

"You're right, of course."

They both sat in a booth in the St. Regis Hotel cocktail lounge and over scotches-and-soda, Marsten told Dave that he would still like to have him at Triton Electronics. The firm's present public relations head, an ex-newspaperman, lacked the proper touch for such work. He was talking of resigning.

"Were paying him seventy-five hundred a year, but we'd go nine thousand for you, Dave."

"I'm making more than that at Worden-Forbes, Bill."

"I know you are. But I also saw the item in the *Herald* about General Wyman angling for a vice-presidency. And I've had a tip that it's the same vice-presidency you're hoping to land. My informant tells me that the General has the inside track."

Dave could have said that he expected to take the inside track away from General Wyman but he was in no mood to do any bargaining. Hurt and despondent over this thing with Nora, he did not feel like talking at all. He simply wanted to be alone.

"How long do I have to give you an answer?"

"When will you know whether or not you'll get the vice-presidency?"

"After the director's meeting, a week from Monday."

"All right, Dave. I'll keep the offer open until then. You call me the following Tuesday. Okay?"

"Okay."

They finished their drinks and Marsten, sensing that Dave did not want to prolong the meeting, said that he had another engagement. They left the hotel together.

As they shook hands, Marsten said, "I don't like to see you miss out on that top spot, Dave. But I want you badly at Triton. Call me—and meanwhile take care of yourself. You really are looking down at the mouth." And Marsten went off.

Dave, having no desire to go home and face Nora, returned to the cocktail lounge and took a stool at the bar. He felt completely empty inside, as though the world had crashed about his shoulders. Nora, he thought bleakly, Nora how could you do this awful tiling? How could you smash everything we had together?

He downed his drink, ordered another. He had a third and then a fourth in quick succession and the barman began to eye him with misgivings. So he went to another bar and after that a third. He drank more in less time than he ever had done before but it did not keep him from thinking of Nora. Of Nora and of that son of a bitch, Brandon Hoyt. Dave left the bar, drove out to the country club and sat a a table, the drink before him forgotten, and tried to analyze the situation, and choose the proper course of action. He had reached the point, he concluded, where he should make a change. He should break away from Worden-Forbes and people like Brandon Hoyt. Never again would he place Nora in a position where she would feel compelled to give herself to a lecherous board member in order to help her husband in his career. With Triton Electronics there would be none of that sort of thing. All he need do, he told himself, was to go to the phone and call Bill Marsten and merely say that he would take the nine-thousand-a-year job. But it would be a big cut in income, which would hurt.

"Hello, darling," a woman said. "You all alone tonight?"

He looked up and saw Penny Austin. Two Penny Austins, actually, for he had drunk so much that he was afflicted with temporary double vision. He blinked several times and she became one—which, he decided, of Penny Austin, was quite enough.

"I'm alone," he said with alcoholic dignity, "by preference."

"But you're not including me out, too, are you, Dave?"

"You and the whole lousy world."

She was unfazed by that. Seating herself, she studied him for a moment. "So you know. And you don't like it."

He stared at her. "Does the whole town know, for chrisesake?"

"Not really. But who was the so-and-so that told you?"

"Nobody told me," he said bitterly. "Nobody tells the husband. I had to eavesdrop on a couple of jerks who were getting a big bang out of it. You alone again?"

"Uh-huh. My ever-lovin' is once more out of town. So if you want to cry on mama's shoulder, well, I've got all night."

"Tramp," he said thickly. "You're all tramps."

"You can't get under my skin, Dave. I've got a real thick hide." Again she studied him and abruptly seemed to make up her mind about something. "Let's go somewhere—and be alone."

Buzzed by his drinks though he was, Dave knew exactly what she meant. She was his for the taking. But right now he didn't want her or any women. Not even Nora. He was disgusted with women, sick of sex.

"I'll drive my car home," Penny said, rising. "You come by and pick me up. Have a cup of coffee instead of that drink. It'll be better for you. Okay?"

He thought of Nora and Brandon Hoyt and the pain was no less than before he'd started drinking. Liquor was no help. Maybe what Penny offered would be.

"I'll think about it while I'm drinking the coffee."

"You do that," she said and turned away.

He watched her leave the lounge, his eyes on her shapely rear. Most of the men in the room stared after her. But he was the one who could have her. He motioned to the waitress, told her to bring him coffee. His mind was not yet made up. But he would do as he had promised–think about it while drinking his coffee.

He was still undecided when he left the lounge and walked to his car. Even driving away from the clubhouse, he did not know if he would pick her up. He had never wanted to cheat on Nora. He had cheated on her only twice in all these years, once before their marriage, for therapy; and once afterward, but through no planning of his own.

The memory of those two sexual adventures came back vividly now as he drove slowly toward Wilshire Heights, toward either his own home or Penny's.

The first time he had cheated on Nora had been two days before their marriage. They had been engaged for two months and before their formal engagement they had had intercourse more or less regularly for nearly a year. Nora had given in to him from the time she admitted to herself that she was in love with him. She had been a virgin until then but no prude. They had understood that they were made for each other, that they would eventually marry. After announcing their engagement, Nora had decided they should wait for "the next time" until their wedding night. It had been as though, by denying themselves, she would now come to their marriage bed at least a halfway virgin. Whatever that was, he reflected sourly.

So he had gone along with her whim, of course. But he had become accustomed to having her and it was increasingly difficult for him to wait. He had begged her to give in—"Just this once," he had urged her on several occasions. He had tried sulking and even getting sore. But Nora had been firm in her resolution of no sex until they were man and wife. She had remained adamant and nothing had broken her down.

He had been aware that he could have borne the situation if he had not been seeing her every evening. But being with her had only increased his difficulty and he had actually suffered. He had been jumpy, on edge, irritable. The Wednesday evening before their wedding, which was set for Saturday, he had pleaded with her for hours to give in. However, she had refused, saying, "And mind you, none of that do-it-yourself stuff, either."

The next day had really been bad. He had been too nervous to sit at his desk, to get any work done. He had felt as though he would crack up if he did not find relief. Then he had remembered the name of a call girl, Helen Barsovitz, with whom a pal of his was friendly. During his lunch hour, he had decided to look her up in the phone book. And there she was listed.

He had said, "Helen you don't know me, but a mutual friend told me about you—Terry Andrews."

"Oh, Terry.—Well, any friend of Terry's is a friend of mine."

"Could I see you this afternoon, Helen?"

"I'm sorry, but I only make evening dates."

"Please, you've got to," he had said desperately. Knowing her rate was twenty dollars, he had plunged on. "I'll give you fifty dollars."

"My, my! You are in a dither, aren't you?"

"Fifty. Please?"

"Well, since you're so set on it. But you'll have to wait an hour before you come up." She laughed softly. "Can you wait that long?"

"Yes, I can wait that long."

He had called her from a phone booth and he was drenched with nervous sweat and shaking violently as he stepped out.

Helen lived in a small, modern apartment building, and when she let him in, Dave was doubly surprised. She was nothing like his idea of a call girl. She was "nice" instead of sexy, a small brunette in a plain green dress. And there were two small children in the tastefully furnished living room with her.

"Come in," she said, smiling. "I'm not alone, as you see. I had trouble getting in touch with my sitter but she's on her way now."

One child was a girl of five, the other a boy of three. They were quiet, well-mannered children sitting politely on the sofa, each with a toy. After asking his name, their mother introduced them. The door chimes sounded and the sitter entered, a stout, pleasant woman of about sixty with whom the children went eagerly. As the three went out, the sitter turned in the doorway, looked from Dave to Helen, and broadly winked.

Helen laughed as the door closed after them. "Kate knows, of course, But it's all right with her—she's an old pro. Would you like a drink?"

"Please," Dave said.

He needed a drink. He was inexperienced in dealing with call girls. He had had a couple of other girls before Nora, but they had been as young and no more expert at love making than himself. This woman seemed as knowledgeable as the most wayward of Eve's daughters and suddenly he felt embarrassed and callow with her. He was fearful that he would not be able to prove himself a man.

But she understood men and seemed to understand him especially. She had a drink with him and talked to get his mind off himself.

"You're probably wondering about me," she said. "This isn't a side of me many men get to see. I never have dates at home because my children come first, really."

She told him that she was married but that her marriage had been a mistake. Her husband, one of those unhappy men who never seem to grow up, had been a yeoman in the Navy. He kept re-enlisting, though she begged him to give it up and take a job and be with her and their children. He was now at sea in the Pacific.

"He comes home less and less often. And you can imagine what sort of life the children and myself would have if I tried to five on what money I get from him."

"They're nice children."

"And I'm determined to have them grow up to be nice adults, too," she said. "They will have at least some advantages." She paused, smiling, "Now I'm curious about you. Why should a young handsome joe like you have to buy it?"

"I'm getting married Saturday."

"Oh? And you want one last fling?"

"Not that. My girl—my fiancée—decided we should stop having each other until our wedding night. It's been two months now."

"Well, that is a new reason." She rose, took his empty glass. She slipped her arms about his neck when he got to his feet, pressed her body to his. "I've got all afternoon. The sitter and the kids won't be back until five. That should be long enough to get you over the jitters." She kissed him. "I'm going to make this afternoon one you'll remember, even when you're on your honeymoon, Dave. You can do anything to me you want, and I'll do anything you want me to do. Come along to bed."

He went with her to her bedroom, his taut nerves already beginning to ease.

And on his honeymoon with Nora, he had remembered—guiltily but with no regret at all—that wonderful, stolen, therapeutic afternoon.

The second time he had been unfaithful was during the third year of his and Nora's marriage. He had not sought a woman that time. She had come to him while he slept.

Worden-Forbes had been about to open its Richmond plant and he had been down there with a dozen of the firm's executives planning the ceremony for the dedication of the new factory. His job was to line up some local VIPs for the affair. He was sharing a hotel suite with Herb Sundersen—two bedrooms and a sitting room. The second night Herb suggested that they pick up a couple of women and take them up to the suite.

Dave wanted no part of it, but Herb, pretty well looped, did bring a woman up with him. Dave had a drink with them, then went to his bedroom. He closed but did not lock the connecting door, and was awakened an hour later by someone getting into bed with him. It was Herb's pickup, and she was nude.

Dave turned on the lamp on the bedside table, stared at her angrily. "Get the hell out of here. I don't want any part of you. Go on—scram!"

She was a big, voluptuous blonde. "Aw, honey, have a heart," she coaxed, rubbing her soft, naked body against him. "That jerk in the other room passed out on me after getting me all steamed up. I've got to have a man. Please—pretty please."

She took his hand, rubbed it over her rounded buttocks, then around to her mounded belly. Desire inflamed him. He could not help himself. He turned off the lamp, threw off his pajamas, seized her and lost himself in her warm, scented flesh. He performed well with her and he had her twice during the night and once in the morning. He felt guilty about it for a long time, even though he had been trapped into it and could not help himself.

So he had cheated on Nora only twice, and neither time because he had wanted to cheat on her.

Now, as he found himself pulling up before the Austin's house, there was Penny coming along the walk. He had come to her without really being aware of it, without actually desiring her. He knew why, of course. He needed to forget his wife's infidelity. Liquor had not brought him forgetfulness; perhaps Penny Austin could.

He reached across the seat and opened the door. "Get in, you redheaded tramp," he said, hating both her and himself.

CHAPTER THIRTEEN

THEY drove across town and entered the Expressway at the Northgate cloverleaf. Dave pushed the Buick up to sixty and for the next twenty-odd miles not a word passed between them. Near the Harrisburg-East Shore entrance to the Pennsylvania Turnpike, he swung off the Expressway to find a motel. They checked in at the first decent- appearing one they saw, a defiant mood causing him to sign the registration card as Mr. and Mrs. David Osborne instead of using a fictitious name.

Once they were in their room, he said, "We should have brought some liquor along."

Penny shook her head. "You've had enough and I don't need any."

He gazed at her without tenderness, with neither pleasure or desire. She was a damn attractive piece and he wondered on many occasions what it would be like to hold her in his arms. Now, hating her because she was a woman and all women were cheats, he felt more like roughing her up, hurting her, than making love to her.

She watched him with a half-amused, half-challenging expression. When he moved toward her, she quickly eluded his reaching hands.

"Let me get my dress off," she said. "I don't want to look as though I went through a war when we leave here."

He waited, watching as she removed her beige sheath, and put it carefully over the back of a chair. She turned toward him, smiling wantonly. She wore no slip, only panties and a bra which barely contained her abundant breasts.

"All right, you. You've wanted it for a long time, so now take it."

"Who said I ever wanted you, you redheaded bitch?"

"Nobody needed to say it. I've seen you looking at this chassis, big boy—plenty of times."

"And so you had to throw it at me, first chance you got."

"You've still got a choice—take it or leave it."

His fingers locked around her left wrist and his other hand clutched her hair in a twisting grip. She tried to get away but he pulled her against him and kissed her roughly. For a moment she submitted, then snapped her teeth hard on his lower lip. He swore with pain and released her.

She laughed at him. "So you're going to take it, are you?"

"Try and stop me."

"I just might. I don't like the mood you're in."

He caught her again, grabbing her about the waist. He felt her bare flesh beneath his hands and was instantly aware of surging passion. She put her hands against his chest, tried to keep him from pulling her to him. Failing in that, she struck him with her fist. He cursed her, slapped her in the face. She reeled backward, off balance and slumped against the foot of the bed. He got his fingers inside her bra and ripped it from her. She came at him fiercely, her fingers hooked, talon-like, her teeth bared, and tried to claw his face. He seized her right arm, spun her about and closed his arms tightly about her from behind. His hands cupping her breasts, he held her close while she strained frantically to break loose. Her breathing was labored and between gasps she spat obscenities at him.

Then she snarled bitterly, "You bastard, you're hurting me because you want to hurt your wife. You're taking it out on me for what she's done."

"What do you expect—tender caresses?"

"I can take anything you can dish out!"

She slammed her head back against his face. Again there was pain for him and he lost his hold on her. She twisted around, tried to knee him in the groin but he caught her upraised knee and toppled her backward onto the bed. He ripped off her panties, and now she wore only white plastic earrings, a matching bracelet, and white pumps. She lay still but her narrowed gray-green eyes watched him closely. The realization came to him that she was just waiting for a chance to kick him.

"Stay like that," he ordered her, "Move a muscle and I'll slug hell out of you."

"Bastard!" she said. "Oh, you filthy bastard, you!"

When he moved back to undress, she kicked off her shoes but made no attempt to get from the bed.

Then she taunted him as he stood naked before her: "What's so special about you that Nora shouldn't have another man if she wants one? Tell me. I certainly can't see for myself!"

He did not reply but moved warily toward her. She lay supine and motionless until he came down upon her, then fought him fiercely, raking his chest with her nails and closing her teeth on his left shoulder. He seized her wrists, forced her arms above her head, and pressed her face to one side with his own. She squirmed beneath him, trying to keep him from his goal. But in a moment he had her helpless and she gasped and went limp.

He took her with a passion fired by his anger and hatred and he brought her quickly to a shuddering peak. He continued his violent assault on her for his own pleasure now, even though she pleaded with him to let her go—crying that she had had enough. But after a few minutes she subsided again. Her body lost its limp submissiveness and once more began to respond. She moaned as with pleasurable agony and wrapped her now freed arms about him. He carried her along with him through soaring passion until, together, at last they reached the crest of sensation. Then came the aftermath of plunging downward into a passionless void. He rolled off her and lay spent beside her.

Minutes passed with neither of them moving or speaking. Then Penny turned toward him and tried to put her arms about him.

"Dave," she whispered. "Dave, it was wonderful!"

He pushed her seeking arms aside and got out of the bed. He dressed quickly and then, standing with his back turned, he lit a cigarette.

"Get up and get dressed," he said. "I want to get out of here."

"All right, darling."

For Penny, she sounded strangely subdued.

They drove the twenty miles back to town in as many minutes, neither one speaking the entire way. Another ten minutes brought them to Wilshire Heights. When they pulled up before her house, he immediately reached across her and opened the door. She turned to him pleadingly.

"Dave, please don't push me out as though I'm a cheap whore. I don't give myself to every man and I do have feelings—just as you do."

He stared at her coldly. 'What do you want now, for God's sake? A promise of undying love?"

"I could do with a promise—a promise that you won't be too rough on Nora. Just remember that she didn't go with Hoyt merely because she wanted another man. She went with him only because she thought she could help to get that vice-presidency for you. Promise me that, Dave. You must have worked off your anger on me. So promise—please!"

"Next you'll be saying you went with me just to get me to make such a promise."

"Maybe I did, in part, because I'm fond of Nora. And maybe I did partly for you, because you needed somebody tonight. You felt alone in the world and—"

"And your being a tramp had nothing to do with it, eh?"

"Maybe my being a tramp did have something to do with it, too. Oh, I'll be honest and admit that I wanted you. But do you promise?"

"Yes, damn it, I promise."

She leaned close, kissed him on the cheek, then got from the car. She closed the door, and looked in at him.

"If you love her, and I know you do, all this foolishness need not be the end of the world, Dave."

"All right, all right."

"Goodnight," she said, and started along the walk.

"Penny."

She faced about. "Yes, Dave?"

"I'm sorry about calling you that name."

"I know you are," she said, and stood watching as he drove away.

At one twenty-seven Dave arrived home. He entered the house reluctantly, knowing that he would quarrel with Nora—and knowing too that he would have to accept the status quo. What was done was done. There was no undoing her infidelity, which, after all, had been committed because she hoped to help him win the job he wanted. Or had she gone with Hoyt for only that reason? Possibly she had really wanted to stray—and had welcomed an excuse. Perhaps she had had a yen for Brandon Hoyt. Exasperated, he swore to himself. A man could not know what really motivated another person's actions—not even those of his own wife.

Dave found Nora in bed but awake and waiting for him. She was lying on her side, propped up on an elbow with a book open beside her. She closed the book, sat up, gazing at him accusingly. Her black hair was prettily tousled. She was wearing a pale yellow nightgown and she was so lovely. He looked away, for looking at her hurt too much. Another man had possessed her and Dave had the absurb feeling that she was now somehow different from the woman he loved.

"Well, you and Bill Marsten did make an evening of it," she said. "He really must have worked on you."

Removing his coat, he said tonelessly, "I spent about twenty minutes with Bill." He went to the closet, placed his coat on a hangar. "I spent the rest of the night going from bar to bar, trying to get stoned."

"Oh? And just why did you feel the need to get stoned?"

He looked directly at her. "I heard about you and Brandon Hoyt."

Nora remained very still, seeming not even to breathe. Her face drained of color, became chalky. After a long moment she lowered her gaze from his and stared at her hands that were clasped on her lap. Then she looked up again, her face stricken.

"You know why I did it, don't you?"

"I know why you think you did it. You convinced yourself you were doing it for me."

"You needed help."

"And you gave yourself to that bastard to get me that help. Do you actually think he'll keep his word—if he gave you his word on anything?"

"I'm hoping he'll keep it, Dave."

"You're hoping, for chrisesake." He removed his shirt, threw it and his tie onto the chaise lounge. "For your information, I have a way to handle Brandon Hoyt—and it'll be my way and no tyours that gets me that job."

"All right, Dave. If you can swing it on your own, I'll be glad. I want you to feel that you've done it on your own. But I was worried. I was scared to death that we would have to give up this house—the plans we've made for Louise and for the future. I didn't want Hoyt. God knows I didn't want to do such a thing. I hated doing it, believe me. I hated every minute of it and—"

"The hell you say," he cut in savagely. "Sex is sex, and you can't tell me you turned frigid just because you went to bed with another man beside me. Damn it, Nora, I never wanted us to be like this. It's a lousy situation for a man to be in."

He removed his T-shirt and Nora, gazing at him, said bitterly, "But your never wanting us to be like this didn't stop you, did it?"

"Just what do you mean by that?"

"Look at yourself. And don't tell me you got those marks pub-crawling. Only a woman leaves marks like those."

He looked down at himself and saw the four long red scratches on his chest from Penny's clawing fingernails. And on his left shoulder was a clearly defined set of teeth marks where Penny had bitten him.

"So I wanted to get even," he said, some part of him wanting to protect Penny. "And I picked up a twenty- dollar whore."

Tears welled in Nora's eyes. "All right. So you had to get even and you picked up a twenty-dollar whore. Just where does all this leave us? What has it to do with us?"

"All I know is that I'll get that damned vice-presidency for us. And I'll get it my way. I've got enough on Brandon Hoyt to make him drop his Air Force pal like a hot rock and back me instead. And that, my cheating little bitch, is more than all your fornication would do in a lifetime."

He turned and strode toward the door.

Frightened, Nora called, "Dave, where are you going?"

"Downstairs to get swacked," he said flatly. "To drink myself blotto and try to forget that you let that bastard lay you."

Nora began to sob painfully. To keep him from hearing, she buried her face in the pillow. She wept with the hurt of knowing that Dave had been with another woman and with fear of what was happening to their marriage.

Sobbing into her pillow until she was exhausted, at last she fell into a troubled, fitful sleep.

In the morning, during the brief interval between getting dressed and Dave's leaving for the plant, Nora saw the pattern of what their marriage was now to be. Dave was civil, even polite, but nothing more. He did not speak one unnecessary word. Their marriage was to be kept a going thing and for appearances' sake they would seem still a devoted couple. But actually they would continue to be as estranged and remote from each other as they were at this moment. Her affair with Brandon Hoyt would not be mentioned again—but it would not be forgotten.

Dave ate his breakfast, said goodbye, and was gone. He left her gripped by a chill feeling of impending disaster.

Clearing the table, Nora found his cigarette lighter beside his coffee cup—the little gold lighter engraved with his initials that she had given him when he had moved into the carpeted office where he now worked. She had wanted to give him something expensive to show how deserving she thought him. That he had forgotten the lighter this morning seemed somehow symbolic of all that was wrong between them. She gave way to the tears that had been so close to the surface since she awoke.

By mid-morning she could no longer bear being alone. She needed someone to talk to, a woman friend, and she had no confidante except Penny Austin, She picked up the phone.

"Penny, it's Nora. Are you busy?"

"I'm never busy, darling. But what's wrong? You sound so strange."

"It's Dave, Penny—he's found out."

"Oh, no."

'I need a shoulder to cry on. Do you mind if I come over?"

"Oh, I wish you would, Nora. I always seem to be running over to your place to see you."

"I'll be there in ten minutes," Nora told her.

Penny came from the house when Nora pulled into the Austin's driveway. She looked, as usual, fresh and happy, untouched by trouble. Envying her, Nora wondered why everything misfired for her while nothing ever seemed to go wrong with Penny's life.

They went around to the flagstone terrace where Penny had coffee ready.

"How bad was it?" the redheaded girl asked as she poured the coffee. "Did Dave give you a rough time?"

"Well, he didn't threaten me with a divorce," Nora said bleakly, "but he was rough when he came home late and half-stoned, slapped me in the face with his accusation. He was mad and said pretty rough things. But the worst part of it was that he'd been with a woman. And that just tore me all to hell."

Penny stared at her. "He told you he'd been with a woman?"

"No. She left marks on him."

"Marks?"

"Whoever she is, she's a scratcher and a biter."

Penny took a swallow of coffee, lit a cigarette, frowned in silence for a time. "You poor kid. What makes it so tough is that you're both such moral people—so puritanical. Both Dave and you magnify the importance of this playing around out of all proportion. But you've got to keep these relatively small missteps from smashing your marriage, Nora. You've just got to."

"We have a pretty badly smashed marriage now, Penny."

"I wish I knew what to tell you to do."

"To make matters worse, my affair with Brandon was probably pointless. Dave said he has his own way to force Brandon to drop General Wyman and back him instead."

"Oh, God—*men!*" Penny snorted. "They're all little-boy show-offs. Dave was just bragging to make himself feel better."

"You really think so, Penny?"

"Honey, I know men," Penny said. "To hear my Bart talk now, you'd think he climbed to his good job all by his own efforts but he's conveniently forgotten that little Penny was really responsible. I can't see Dave or anybody else forcing Brandon Hoyt into anything."

At ten-thirty that morning Dave had caught up with his most pressing work. He had Miss Marvin get Harvey Ward on the phone.

"Harv, did you talk it over with Lucy?"

"Yeah, I talked to her about it."

Dave waited, holding his breath. How weird, he thought, that my entire future depends upon a drab little housewife like Lucy Ward.

Harvey Ward went on, "She's all for the idea. I always thought that dame was more than a little wacky, and now I know it."

Dave began to breathe again. "Good for Lucy. I'll have to send her some flowers or something to show my appreciation of a very astute young woman."

"Just don't send candy," Ward said. "She's putting on enough weight. When do you want the—the thing, Dave?"

"Can I buy you lunch again today?"

"You can buy me lunch any day, pal."

"See you at twelve. You can give me die thing then."

"Right, Dave."

Dave put down the phone, leaned back in his chair, and frowning, lit a cigarette. He did not feel as good about his plan now, he told himself, as he should. The prospect of cutting the high-and-mighty Brandon Hoyt down to size should be pleasant to contemplate. Getting the man's support for the vice-presidency should seem sweet revenge for Hoyt's plan to put that Air Force friend into the office. But Dave could not feel smug about it. And he knew why: Because Brandon Hoyt had cuckolded him and even while the man was crawling, he would secretly be laughing at Dave.

Still, the photostat of that letter was a weapon powerful enough to force Hoyt to back him. His support, together with that of John Fletcher, should win Dave the vice-presidency hands down.

He asked Miss 'Marvin to call Dawson's, the florist where he had an account, and have some flowers delivered to Mrs. Harvey Ward.

The small gesture would tell Lucy that he was not unappreciative—that he would not forget.

Then, reflectively, he wondered why a man could not further his career without women being involved in the process. That was, he decided, a sad commentary on the state of modern big business.

CHAPTER FOURTEEN

THE weekend was no better than Nora had expected. Dave and she went to the club Saturday evening and made a public pretense that all was well between them. But they were uncomfortable in each other's presence. Their attempts at conversation were awkward, almost embarrassing. Dave drank too much and when they left for home, she had to do the driving.

They spent Sunday visiting Louise at Camp Wee-ni- toka. The child again said she wanted to go home but this time Nora felt sure she did not mean it. Louise was in a happier mood. Under questioning, she reluctantly admitted that some of the girls now seemed more friendly. As they walked about the grounds, one little girl stopped to chat with them; she was a child whose angelic expression was belied by the pixyish gleam in her blue eyes. This was Gretchen and Nora guessed that she was the one selected to break down Louise's reserve. And Gretchen was doing a good job, for in her presence Louise talked and laughed in normal little-girl fashion.

After they had talked to Gretchen, Louise suggested a walk in the woods. They agreed, and Dave said, with a heavy attempt at humor, that he hoped they wouldn't get lost.

"Nobody gets lost, Daddy," Louise told him. "That's silly. In all the time I've been here, nobody's ever been lost."

They walked a long way through the dense woodland, Louise saying that they were heading in a westerly direction. She proudly pointed out that she could tell this from the position of the afternoon sun and from their shadows being behind them. After perhaps an hour they came to a weed grown dirt road. The land beyond this road was out of bounds for the young people of Camp Wee-ni-toka, Louise informed her parents. The counselor Miss Leland, never took the girls of her group one step across the road that marked the camp boundary.

"But you could take me just a little farther," Louise said. "Will you, Daddy—Mommy?"

Dave said, "Well, just a little farther, honey."

So they went a little farther and found the Secret Cave, as the child immediately named the deep hollow beneath a rock ledge in the side of a bluff. In a sizeable area before the bluff only grass and bushes grew. Louise wondered at the lack of trees, and when she insisted upon an explanation, Nora made up a story.

"Once upon a time," Nora said, "long before the white man came to this country, a family of Indians—a father Indian, a mother Indian and a little girl Indian—lived where Camp Wee-ni-toka now stands. One day their wigwam was destroyed by some bad Indians. So the little family set out through the forest to find another place to build a new wigwam. Well, they walked and walked but the forest got thicker and thicker. They just couldn't find a place to live. But then—"

"—then they found this place," Louise broke in. "And lived in the Secret Cave."

"No, not quite," Nora told her. "The way the story goes, Father Indian and Mother Indian became very tired and oh-so very discouraged. They lost all hope of finding a new place to five. But Little Girl Indian said, 'Maybe if we pray to the Great Spirit'—which is what they called God—'He will help us.'"

"And the Great Spirit found this place for them?"

"Well, yes," Nora said. "But not right away, for the Great Spirit helped only those Indians who also helped themselves.

The Indian family asked Him to help them find a place to build their new home. Suddenly the sky grew black, black as night in the middle of the day, and there was wind and thunder and lightning. There was going to be rain, too. The Indian family had no shelter. They started running, looking for a place to protect them from the storm. Just before the rain came they found this Secret Cave, even though in those days trees grew right up to the mouth.

"And here, inside the cave, they huddled with their possessions. And a good thing, too, for the strong wind blew down all the trees in front of the cave. Then—"

"So that's why there are no trees here!" Louise exclaimed.

"Yes, that's why," Nora said, laughing. "But I told you that the Great Spirit helped only those Indians who helped themselves. When the storm passed, the three Indians realized what a nice place this would be for a home if they cleared away all those fallen trees. So they began working. They worked for days and days, clearing away the fallen trees. Then they had a nice yard in front of their cave and Little Girl Indian played there. Birds came to be her friends, and some rabbits, and even a little deer. But the strange part was that the trees never grew here again."

"Oh, that's a wonderful story!" Louise said, her face aglow. "Even though you made it up!"

Nora laughed, and so did Dave.

And just for a little while the three were happy again.

It did not last, of course. After they had taken Louise back to camp and were driving to Lanford, Dave and Nora were as much estranged as they had been before seeing their daughter. They stopped for dinner at a restaurant on the way home but Nora only picked at * her food. When they reached home at eight o'clock, Dave suggested they go to the club again. She pleaded a headache and told him to go alone if he wished. Then she felt hurt when he did go alone. Unhappy and depressed, she went to bed at ten o'clock, taking a sleeping pill.

Monday was a blue day, but in the afternoon Penny Austin phoned and asked if Nora would like to drive to Baltimore and go shopping. Nora said she would very much like to go. She hoped the trip would take her mind off her despondency about her marriage, at least for a few hours. She left a note for Dave, telling where she and Penny were going and that she might be a little late in getting home.

Dave found the note on his study desk when he got home at five-thirty. He read it with annoyance. Despite their estrangement, he wanted Nora there when he got home because the house seemed empty without her. Furthermore, he did not like her being away with Penny Austin. He wondered what Penny was trying to do. Sooner or later Penny would be sure to let her tongue slip and Nora would learn that Penny was the woman he had been with the other night. Damn Penny, anyway!

Well, no wonder he was in such a foul mood. He had had a bad day, starting from the moment he had learned that General Lyle Wyman, USF Retired, was in town, a guest of the Brandon Hoyts. Then during the afternoon Hoyt had taken the general through the plant and the offices, including Dave's. When the pair walked in unannounced—for Miss Marvin had been away from her desk—Dave had been possessed by a wild, compulsive urge to slug Hoyt. He had to use all his will power to smile pleasantly and acknowledge the introduction to the general. The thought had kept running through his mind: This is the man who had your wife … This is the man who had your wife. He had found himself hating Hoyt as he had never before hated anybody.

As for Wyman, Dave had been impressed to a degree—as he would have been by any top flight military man. Wyman was tall and slender, with iron-gray hair and bronzed skin. Even in civvies he held himself stiff and straight. He was austere in manner, clipped of speech. With each utterance he had seemed to imitate a more famous general's pronouncement: "I shall return!"

But impressed or not by the visitor's military personality and bearing, Dave would have challenged the general's ability, given the opportunity, to handle this office. And as the two had left Dave to continue their sightseeing tour, he thought sourly: Get back to the golf course, pal, where all retired generals belong.

The visit had left him in a depressed mood. He had had in his pocket the photostat that would certainly end Hoyt's sponsorship of Wyman. He had had it since noon, Friday, when Harvey Ward rather reluctantly had handed the copy to him.

That afternoon he had planned to have Miss Marvin call Hoyt's secretary and make an appointment for him. Then he would confront the man with the photostatic evidence of his taking kickbacks and his serious breach of that important company rule. But back at his office after lunch, he had been reluctant to put the call through. He had let the afternoon get away from him and today, Monday, he had still hesitated to seek an appointment. He had begun to wonder if he lacked the nerve to carry through his plan, or if he had scruples against blackmail.

So now, he told himself: Tomorrow … I'll see him first thing in the morning …

But next morning, Tuesday, he waited too long, and not until nearly noon did he ask Miss Marvin to call Hoyt's secretary. A moment later she told him over the intercom that the appointment was set for next Monday afternoon at four o'clock.

"That's the best I could do, Mr. Osborne. Mr. Hoyt was in his office for only an hour this morning. And he won't be in again the rest of the week. He's going out of town."

Jolted, Dave silently cursed the subconscious motive that had kept him from contacting Hoyt earlier. The directors' meeting was scheduled for ten o'clock and an appointment with the man at four would be too late. More, it would disastrous.

"Listen, Hilda," he told Miss Marvin. "Get me his secretary. I want to talk to her. And by the way, what's her name?"

"Kulaski, Mr. Osborne."

"Well, let me talk to her."

A moment later she told him that she had Miss Kulaski on the phone.

He said, "Miss Kulaski, it's very important that I talk to Mr. Hoyt before the board meeting on Monday. Important to him as well as to me. See if you can't work me in early in the morning, won't you?"

"I'm sorry, Mr. Osborne, but Mr. Hoyt's schedule is filled for Monday morning. I could squeeze you in at nine, if you don't need more than, say, ten minutes."

"I won't need more than two minutes, Miss Kulaski."

"Very well. I'll put you down for nine."

Dave thanked her and set down the phone. He felt shaken, unnerved. This was cutting it pretty close. Still, it might work out better this way. He would give Hoyt the jolt just before the meeting and the man would be reeling under it when he went to the board room. Yes, that might be better.

General Wyman's visit to Lanford and to Worden- Forbes was given adequate press coverage, even though the publicity was not arranged by Dave's department but by Brandon Hoyt. Both the Monday evening *Bulletion* and the Tuesday morning *Herald* carried interviews and pictures of Wyman. The general had denied to reporters that his visit to Worden-Forbes meant that he was considering joining the corporation as an executive. He was quoted as saying he had no plans for the future other than to live on the nearby farm that he had bought several years ago. His farm was close to the Idlewild Golf Club, and he hoped to get in a great deal of golf.

Nora read the publicity given the general and she felt sick at heart. She was completely convinced now that Brandon Hoyt would not keep his promise to her. He had never intended to keep it when he made it, she told herself. He had simply used her, made a fool of her. She came very close to giving way to tears over the way she had been misused and for the wrong being done to Dave.

Again she turned to Penny Austin, needing to cry on someone's shoulder. And Penny, inviting her to lunch at the Red Mill on Harverford Road, was understanding and sympathetic.

"Well, you never did really expect Brandon to keep his word," Penny said as they sipped daiquiris. "But that doesn't make it any easier to accept, I know. How is Dave taking it?"

"Hard. Or I imagine he is, at least. He doesn't talk about it. He doesn't talk anything over with me these days." Nora's voice was unsteady, and she had to blink away tears. "We're just two strangers sharing the same house, Penny. He doesn't say one word more to me than is absolutely necessary. And I wouldn't dare bring up this thing."

"One thing sure, he was just talking through his hat when he said he could force Brandon to back him. As I was sure he was."

"I suppose so."

"I wish I knew what to tell you to do."

"I wish you did, too," Nora said bleakly.

The waitress returned and they ordered lunch. Nora asked for a salad of fruit and cottage cheese but Penny, who never seemed to worry about her figure, said she would have the veal scallopine with noodles. They talked little; Nora was lost in a gloomy reverie and Penny was in one of her rare thoughtful moods. But later, after ordering dessert—for Nora a lime sherbet and Penny a hot- fudge sundae—they resumed their discussion.

"Maybe Dave does have a way to force Brandon to back him," Penny said, "then, being Dave, he just hasn't the nerve to make use of it."

"But what do you think Dave's scheme could be, Penny?"

Penny shrugged. "I haven't a single, solitary idea. I wish I had. You couldn't sound him out, could you?"

Nora shook her head. "I wouldn't dare. You just don't know how it is between us. If I even mentioned Brandon Hoyt, there would be a battle. It preys on Dave's mind that Brandon was my—my lover."

"Then there's only one thing to do."

"What, Penny? What could we do?"

"Not we, just I. I could see Mark Hammond."

"Oh, Penny—would you?"

"For you, yes," Penny said. "You and Dave are like a couple of lost, frightened children. Somebody's got to help you, and I'd never forgive myself if I didn't try. Anyway, Mark Hammond will arrive in town a day or two before the directors' meeting and he always calls me, even if he doesn't want a date. Poor Mark's dating days are about over now because he's getting on in years. But when he calls, I'll ask him to meet me. And I'll plead your—and Dave's—case."

"Penny, you're a doll—a real pal."

"I'm just an old softie," Penny said, smiling wryly. "Next, I'll be taking in stray cats and dogs. But don't get your hopes too high. I can go only so far with Mark; he's not indebted to me, or at least he doesn't feel that he is. I'll tell him what the situation is between Dave and Brandon and try to make him see Dave is experienced where that Air Force character is not. That's as far as I can go without stepping out of bounds. But if Mark should feel that Dave will make a better vice-president than General Wyman, he'll squash Brandon like a bug. One thing always comes first with old Mark, and that's Worden-Forbes."

"Penny, I think you'll save Dave and me," Nora said, frantically clutching at this last straw of hope. "If you do, I'll love you forever."

Penny laughed. "Please, darling, I'm not like that. I've never been double-gaited in my life."

"Oh, I didn't mean—"

"I know you didn't," the redheaded girl said. "I was just having my little joke."

Penny pleaded another engagement when they left the restaurant but she did not hurry away when they reached their separate cars on the Red Mill parking lot. She got behind the wheel of her convertible and waited until Nora drove off in her station wagon. Then she got from her car and went to the telephone booth at the side of the old stone building. She called Worden- Forbes and asked for Mr. David Osborne, Public Relations.

"One moment, please …"

Another feminine voice said, "Mr. Osborne's secretary. Who is calling?"

Secretaries, Penny thought and made a face. They guarded their bosses more staunchly than wives did their husbands.

"Mrs. Bart Austin."

"One moment, Mrs. Austin. I'll see if Mr. Osborne is in his office."

"You know damned well he's in his office, dearie," Penny said. "You just put him on now, you hear?"

Miss Marvin did not answer, but in a moment Dave said guardedly, "Hello, Mrs. Austin."

"This is Penny, Dave. Let's not play games. If you can't trust your secretary not to listen in, you'd better get one you can trust. Dave, I've got to see you."

Sounding annoyed, he said, "I'm pretty busy, Penny."

"Well, just don't be too busy. I've come from having lunch and an interesting discussion with Nora. Now I've got to see you."

"Well ... All right."

"Make it five o'clock, at that place east of town—the Florida Room. Okay, Dave?"

"Okay," he said grudgingly.

Leaving the booth and returning to her car, Penny decided that she did not quite understand herself. She sat there for a moment, wondering why she was going to all this bother. It was not at all like her to help others. She was essentially selfish, and believed that charity began and ended at home. Never in her life had she gone out of her way to help anyone. But here she was, in a dither to help the Osbornes.

Though seldom self-analytical, she did try to puzzle out this act of unselfishness on her part. She was fond of Nora. She had never been as friendly with another woman. Penny was no woman's woman, that was for sure, and she never had been. But Nora liked her and she liked Nora. Why that should be, Penny had no idea, for they had little in common, actually. Nora was pretty much of a prude, and she—well, she was just the opposite.

Still, she liked Nora and held a sort of protective feeling toward her. That was a part of it. Dave was another part, she supposed. It was odd how she felt about Dave Osborne. Usually when she had had a man other than her husband, she forgot the relationship immediately after leaving his arms. But she had not forgotten that night at the motel with Dave. She had told him then that being with him had been wonderful, and she had meant it. He had given her the most excitingly pleasurable hour she had ever experienced. He might not be much of a business go-getter but as a lover he was something special. True, he had taken her in anger and maybe that had made it more exciting.

However he had taken her, she had enjoyed him more than any man she had ever had and, she wryly admitted to herself, that statement covered a wide territory. But she was not able to forget Dave. So that fact, too, must be behind her wanting to help the Osbornes.

Whatever her motives, she didn't want to see their lives completely smashed. They were fouled up enough already, poor kids.

Penny drove into town, left the convertible on a parking lot and spent the early part of the afternoon in the stores. She made but one purchase, a two-strand set of orchid beads with matching earrings. She paid twenty-two dollars plus tax, an outlandish price for something she would wear only a few times. But she had felt an urge to buy something and she saw really nothing she needed or cared to have. She had reached the point at which shopping was no longer a thrilling and novel past-time, as it had been in the old hungry days when Bart and she had lived on a tight budget.

At four-thirty she walked to the parking lot, got in her convertible and drove west through town. She felt a rising excitement because of the prospect of seeing Dave again and wondered if she wanted a rematch with him. Would she have another date with him, realizing—as she now did—that Nora was her one woman friend? She did not know the answer to that.

The Florida Room, on Route 30, was a squat, white, windowless building with a pair of phony royal palms out front to supplement the subtropical decor inside. She parked the convertible among the half dozen cars already there and went into the cocktail lounge. Taking a stool at the bar, she ordered a daiquiri and almost immediately a Latin type right out of *The Untouchables* tried to move in on her.

"Blow, Joe," she said, freezing all over him. "Blow, or I yell to the management."

He gave her a scowl that would have done a hoodlum proud, but moved back to his stool farther along the bar.

She lit a cigarette, took a sip of her drink, and then, promptly at five, Dave arrived. He, too, was wearing a scowl.

Taking the stool to her right, he said, low-voiced, "Damn it, Penny, what are you trying to do, mess things up for me more than they already are?"

"Now, why would I do such a thing, darling?"

The barman came and Dave asked for a scotch on the rocks.

Then he turned back to her. "Seeing Nora all the time, you're sure to give it away—about us, I mean."

"She already knows you were with a woman that night, remember."

"She doesn't know the woman was you."

"Would that bother her more?"

"You know it would. She thinks of you as a friend. Nora's pretty naïve about some things."

"So are you, darling," Penny said. "Let's have a little privacy for this conference, shall we?"

They took their drinks to a booth. Dave got out cigarettes, gave her one and took one for himself. He lit both with his lighter. He was still scowling and watching her warily.

"Knock off the grudge, for Pete's sake," she told him. "I didn't ask you here to make a pass at you. I want to talk."

"About what?"

"About you," Penny said. She drained her glass. "Buy me another, lover."

Dave downed his own drink before signaling the waitress. When their second round came, Penny said, "I'm going to say something I had not intended to say, Dave, but I think I'd better lay it on the line for you right now, so here goes: You're being completely unfair. Sure Nora did something that hurt you, but she did it for you—for the future of you both. She didn't stray because of any natural inclination on her part. She—"

"Cut it out, Penny. I've heard that record too many times."

She ignored that. "It's even-steven between you. You squared accounts when you had me. So why the grudge against her?"

Dave did not reply.

"All right, clam up. But you're being damned rotten unfair to her."

"If you've said it all, let's break this up."

"I haven't got around to saying what I came to say," she told him. "You told Nora that you have a way to force Brandon Hoyt to drop his Air Force pal and to back you. Were you just bragging?"

"No, I wasn't just bragging."

"So? What have you got on him?"

"Penny, it's none of your business."

"I'm going to help you, Dave—in spite of your nasty mood."

"How?"

"Did you ever hear that Mark Hammond, chairman of the board, is an old and good friend of mine?"

"I'm not exactly deaf to gossip."

"Well, goody for you. Anyway, I'm going to see Mark before the board meeting—to go to bat for you. But I've got to have some specific information, some facts, to get you beyond first base. Right now, all I've got is the argument that I'm fond of the Osbornes and think you deserve the vice-presidency, and that's not much to sell Mark. So if you do have something that will smear Brandon Hoyt in Mark's eyes, that will make this operation a lot easier for me, and for you, too, will you give, or must I go to Mark empty-handed?"

Dave's face was dark with anger. "Dammit, Penny, just keep out of my affairs. I'm fed up with women who try to excuse their sleeping around because they're "helping someone,' for God's sake. Do it for Bart if he puts up with it, but don't do it for me. I can't take that phony stuff."

He swallowed the rest of his drink, slammed the glass down on the formica table top and got up from the booth. He stood bitterly gazing down at her. "I'll tell you what I told Nora. I'm getting that vice-presidency and getting it strictly on my own. Not through any of her two-timing "help'—or any of yours. And that's it."

"Dave, don't go," Peggy begged. "Please don't go."

But he strode away and out the door.

Penny sat there in the midst of her shattered good intentions, telling herself that she was a fool and that she should have known better. You simply could not reason with anyone like Dave Osborne. He would try to bull it through alone and naturally he would mess things up for himself and Nora. Penny was quite sure that he did have something on Brandon Hoyt and she was equally sure that he lacked the nerve to make use of it. She would not pity him when that Air Force general got the vice-presidency but she would feel sorry for Nora. She sighed, finished her drink, then picked up her purse and left the booth.

About to turn away, she noticed that Dave had left his cigarettes and lighter on the table. She picked them up and put them in her purse, having no idea when she would have a chance to give them to him. This was probably the last time she would ever be alone with him. The thought saddened her.

For in one way, at least, Dave Osborne was very much a man.

CHAPTER FIFTEEN

To Nora's despair, the breach between Dave and her widened during the next few days. Dave did not come home until late Tuesday night and when he did arrive he was well stoned. He offered neither explanation nor apology for his late arrival or his condition. He merely stared in silent accusation at Nora as he stalked stiffly through the living room on his way upstairs.

In the morning he looked deathly ill with a hangover and again had nothing to say to her. He was no longer being polite or even civil.

As she was about to go to the garage, she found the courage to say, "Dave, please—is this because you think I've done something wrong again? If you do, it's all in your imagination. You've got to believe that!"

"Quit nagging at me," he said angrily. "I'll be damned if I'm going to be nagged at."

And with that, he drove off to the office.

Wednesday evening he came home early but was still in an ugly temper. He ate little at dinner and then spent the evening drinking alone. She had been rebuffed that morning and did not try to get to him that evening. Discouraged, she concluded that any attempt to break down the wall between them was useless.

Thursday morning was no better and Thursday night he did not come home until nearly one o'clock. He had been drinking again and he looked tormented. Nora was badly frightened and dreaded to think how this nightmare would end. Friday morning, after he had left the house, she wept for him, for them both. She was convinced now that her affair with Brandon Hoyt was only a part of the reason for Dave's behavior. The other part, she felt sure, was his gnawing fear that he would not get the vice-presidency. He was being torn apart and to Nora it seemed that he was slowly destroying them both.

In desperation, she put through a call to Brandon Hoyt. As usual, she got his secretary and had to give her name.

"I'm sorry, Mrs. Osborne," the secretary said, "but Mr. Hoyt is out of town and won't be in his office until Monday morning." And then, slyly: "Didn't Mr. Osborne tell you?"

"Perhaps he did," Nora said, "and it slipped my mind, Thank you, anyway."

She put down the phone, her desperation now a frantic thing. She had hoped to beg Brandon, humbly and abjectly, to give Dave his support, offering in return to do anything he wanted. But she was denied even the chance to so demean herself.

There was still Penny, of course, and her promise to talk to Mark Hammond on Dave's behalf. But Penny had not phoned or stopped around and she did not answer when Nora phoned her. Penny, too, must be away ... She picked up the phone again, dialed the Austin's number. Her hands were trembling violently. If Penny had forgotten to see Mark Hammond, all was lost.

This time, however, Penny answered.

"I'm so glad I caught you in," Nora said. "I've been trying and trying to get you."

"I only got home an hour ago," Penny said. "I ran up to New York for a couple of days with Bart to a convention. He's back in Dayton again and won't be home until the middle of next week. . . How are things with you, Nora?"

"Bad, Penny. Worse than ever."

"Dave's still being the heavily wronged husband?"

Nora said that Dave and she were becoming more and more estranged. "He's drinking heavily all the time. He's hardly ever at home and he won't talk to me at all now. At first I thought he suspected me of—of cheating again. But now I think he's broken up because lie's convinced he won't get the vice-presidency. I tried to call Brandon Hoyt but his secretary says he's out of town and won't be back until Monday morning."

"And this board meeting is Monday?"

"Yes."

"Well, it's a cinch that Dave won't have time to force Brandon into backing him—even if he does have something on that character."

"I've lost hope, Penny. Unless you …

"I haven't forgotten," Penny said. "I'll keep my promise. Mark Hammond is in town at the Harrison and I spoke to him on the phone before I went to New York. I'm seeing him this evening at seven, for a talk. So I'll give it the old college try, Nora. I'll do my best."

"Thanks, Penny. You don't know how grateful I am."

"As I said before, don't get your hopes up too high. I can only tell Mark how deserving you and Dave are, and that really doesn't carry too much weight. If I knew what Dave had on Brandon, I could tell the old boy. If Dave's got something really serious, Mark might go after Brandon's scalp at the board meeting. But I don't suppose there's any way to make Dave tell what it is."

"No way that I know, Penny."

"Too bad. But I'll do my best, and you—well, you keep your fingers crossed."

"You'll call me right after you've seen Mr. Hammond?"

"As soon as I leave him," Penny promised. " 'Bye now."

Nora said goodbye and put down the phone. She was unsure of whether or not to hope. Penny seemed not at all certain she could influence Hammond. If Penny failed now, it could mean real disaster. Dave was showing a weakness she had never suspected and she feared that if he failed to win the vice-presidency, he would have lost the will to try again for promotion. He seemed to be going to pieces even now. And if that were actually the case, could he ever again get hold of himself? She could see him, her beloved Dave, wasting himself, chained forever to some mediocre job, like his friend, Harv Ward. Oh, no—not that, she thought in despair.

She could not know if Dave would be home early, but she made her preparations for dinner. She removed two steaks from the freezer, got together the ingredients for a tossed salad, cutting them to size in the olivewood salad bowl. That done, she went upstairs for her bath. She put on a sheer, pale blue dress, white pumps, and white plastic jewelry. She did her hair and her face with extra care, which took more makeup than usual. Like Dave, she was showing signs of the strain they were under and her color was not good. There were blue black smudges beneath her eyes.

Just before five-thirty, Dave's usual time to arrive home, she was so on edge that she felt the need of a drink. She placed ice cubes in a shaker, added the makings for a daiquiri. She shook the mixture briefly, poured it into a cocktail glass. Sipping the daiquiri, she went to the living room and stood at the picture window. Far down Elm Drive, a car appeared but it turned in at the Jenkens' driveway. Another car came in sight but that was not Dave's either. She knew by the time she had finished the daiquiri that this was another evening she would spend alone. Depressed and sorry for herself, Nora returned to the kitchen and made another daiquiri. She ate a few crackers with pineapple cheese spread while drinking the second cocktail and that was her dinner. Presently she made a third daiquiri. The drinks were making her lightheaded without lifting her spirits.

Penny called much sooner than Nora had expected. When the phone rang at twenty minutes past seven Nora's first thought was that Penny had been unable to get anywhere with Mark Hammond.

"Didn't it work out, Penny?" she asked.

"It's too early to tell," Penny said. "I spoke my piece and Mark's being nice about it. That's why I'm calling so soon. Are you alone, Nora?"

"Yes. Why?"

"Mark would like to talk with you. I think you should come and join us. You can tell him far better than I can just why Dave is the man for the job."

"I'll come, of course."

"Can you make it right away?" Penny said. "I have a date and can't stay here much longer."

"I'll leave now."

"Good," Penny said. "We're in the cocktail lounge at the Harrison. 'Bye now."

Nora put down the phone and hurried to her bedroom to check her makeup and run a comb through her hair. She gave herself a quick inspection in the full-length mirror, decided that her dress would do, snatched up her purse and rushed down to the garage. She reached midtown in fifteen minutes, then spent ten more finding a parking lot three blocks from the Harrison. The hurried walk to the hotel left her breathless and flushed as she entered the lobby.

Pausing just inside the cocktail lounge, she tried to let her eyes adjust to the semidarkness but Penny saw her and waved. As Nora approached the booth, Mark Hammond rose so that she could seat herself. Once she was settled and he sat beside her, Penny introduced them in her breezy manner.

"Nora, my good friend Mark. . . Mark, my good friend Nora."

Smiling, Nora looked directly at Mark Hammond for the first time.

He was a big man, a giant of a man, an outdoors type with a deeply weathered face. A rim of silver hair surrounded his massive bald head. He was in his sixties, but his smile was youthful and his bright blue eyes alert and knowing. Nora could see at once that he had been a handsome man, was still a handsome man, in a rugged, well-aged fashion and he radiated a sense of virility that had an immediate impact upon her. Here is a real man, she reflected.

"Nice of you to come, Nora," he said, offering his hand. "You're every bit as lovely as Penny said."

She gave him her hand and had it swallowed in the vastness of his. He held it a little longer than was necessary, smiling at her while his knowing blue eyes appraised her, as they had doubtlessly appraised a thousand women before her.

"What would you like to drink?" he asked, finally releasing her hand.

'I've already had my quota," she said. "But since this is an occasion—well, I'd like a daiquiri, please."

"Another for you, Penny?" he asked.

Penny shook her head. "I've got to rush. I'll finish this one, then leave you two to talk things over. I'm awfully sorry but I do have this other engagement."

Penny finished her drink soon after Nora was served her daiquiri, then picked up her cigarettes and lighter and dropped them into her purse. Nora noticed the gold fighter and thought how like Dave's it was. Only after the redhead had gone did the thought strike her that she had never seen Penny carry a fighter before; she had always used matches. Then the lighter must be Dave's—the one she had given him to celebrate his new job.

But when and how had Penny gotten the costly gadget? Nora could guess but she hated to believe the obvious answer. Why, Penny was her friend. She would not be having an affair with Dave. Surely, he could not have been with Penny that night—and perhaps since. Penny could not—would not—be on her way to meet him now. Repeatedly Nora kept telling herself that her fears were foolish; then she realized that Mark Hammond was talking to her and she had not caught one word he had said. She tried to rid her mind of these dark thoughts and listen to him.

"I doubt if your husband has anything on Brandon Hoyt," he was saying. "Brandon's too foxy to let anybody maneuver him into a tough spot. Besides, it seems to me that if your Dave has any valid evidence that Brandon has been cutting corners, he would have used it."

"Dave does have something, Mr. Hammond," Nora said. "I know he has. He doesn't say things he doesn't mean. He's not—well, a bluffer or a liar. If only you'd talk to him, I'm sure he'd tell you what it is."

"Oh, I don't think it will be necessary for me to see him."

"You mean—?" Nora said, feeling her heart give a wild, hopeful lurch.

"I mean," he said, smiling at her, "that I'm in a mood to let you convince me that Dave, and not some retired Air Force general, should fill that vice-presidency."

Nora went rigid, for his hand moved from atop the table to her thigh.

"Why don't we go upstairs to Worden-Forbes' suite?" Hammond went on. "This is a matter that needs privacy to discuss properly."

CHAPTER SIXTEEN

His oversized hand moved slowly back and forth over her thigh in a sensuous caress. Nora inwardly shuddered and wanted to cry out: Stop this, you nasty-minded old man, but the reasoning part of her mind warned her to keep silent. One wrong move and she would irreparably destroy not only Dave's future but hers and Louise's as well.

His fingers started to knead the soft, smooth flesh of her thigh. Her mind raced frantically this way and that like a mouse in a maze, seeking some way of escape. But she knew that this was a trap from which she herself had blocked every exit—unless she wanted to throw everything away. What did it matter? she thought bleakly. Dave was involved with Penny and she had lost him forever. But there was no need for her to lose everything else.

How could she be sure, though? She had gone through this sort of thing with Brandon Hoyt and his promise had turned out to be only a ghastly joke. How could she be sure that this man's word was any better than Hoyt's? Because Penny had said he kept his promises? Penny, she thought bitterly. Her dear, loyal friend, Penny.

"Penny—she set this up for you, didn't she?"

"For me?" Hammond said, looking surprised. "My impression was that she set it up for you."

"How can I be sure you'll keep your word?"

"My word is as good as my bond, my dear. Penny must have told you that I kept my promise to her."

"She did. But it was a long time ago that you helped her husband. You could have changed since then."

"I've changed in some ways," he said, smiling wryly. "But not in that way."

'You'll see that Dave gets the vice-presidency?"

"I will."

"You can swing it, even over Brandon Hoyt's objections?"

"I can shut him up before he even starts to talk," he said confidently. "I have the board in the palm of my hand."

Nora reached for what was left of her daiquiri. She drank it down and stared bleakly at the empty glass while his insistent hand still caressed her thigh. She told herself that he was not really touching her—not the real Nora. She could let him use her body, up there in the ninth-floor suite, but she would hold her inner self aloof from it. She would not let him reach her, no matter how much he caressed her. She would be merely an empty, unfeeling vehicle for his physical pleasure, and would reject the taint of his maleness even as he labored over her in panting quest of sensual satisfaction.

"All right," she said, and was surprised by the steadiness of her voice. "All right, I'll go."

"Good," he said, and now took his hand away. "If you'd rather not have people see us go up together, I'll go first. The suite number is—"

She thought of Dave and Penny, perhaps together this very moment. Dave lost in Penny's lush, lovely flesh—because he wanted to be.

She said, "If you're not ashamed for us to be seen together, why should I be?"

He gazed at her with surprise for a moment, then shrugged.

"All right," he said. "Let's be on our way."

He left the booth and she picked up her purse and followed. As they walked together across the lobby toward the elevators she felt dwarfed by his hugeness. He was slightly stooped, in the manner of many enormously tall men, but even so he must have stood six-feet-four. It seemed to her that the eyes of everyone in the lobby were on them, knowing where they were going and exactly for what purpose. She held her head high, thinking: Go on and stare. If you've never seen a whore, you're seeing one now. A sob welled up in her throat.

As they entered an elevator, Hammond said, "Ninth floor, son."

"Yes, sir, Mr. Hammond." The door slid closed, and they were whisked upward.

Stepping from the elevator, Nora thought, Welcome to the Ninth Floor Club, darling. The initiation is quite simple, merely a matter of taking off your panties and climbing into the hay.

She walked beside the huge old man along the corridor to the suite. He produced a key, unlocked and pushed the door open, moving aside to let her enter first. She hesitated, held back by a sudden revulsion until his hand closed on her arm and its vast strength moved her into the sitting room of the suite.

"A drink?" he asked, going to the bar in the corner. "I'm having one."

"Yes, thanks," she said tonelessly.

The more numb she became, the better.

He returned to her with two tall drinks, handed her one, then, his hand gripping her arm again, led her into one of the adjoining bedrooms. He shut the door and Nora felt herself a prisoner in a remote, ugly corner of the world where she would be soiled forever. In this large room, with the two double beds and chaise lounge, Nora guessed, the visitors must spend most of their time in a horizontal position.

She took a fast swallow of her drink, then placed the tumbler and her purse on the bureau, removed her plastic costume jewelry, her dress and slip. She turned to him in panties and bra. He stood sipping his drink, feasting his eyes on her partially nude body.

"As I said downstairs," he told her, "I've changed in some ways. Age has caught up with me, to my sorrow. Unfortunately, I seem to have more failures than successes with women nowadays. This may be another failure."

"If it is, you can't hold me to blame," Nora said. "You'll still keep your word?"

"I'll still keep my word," he said. "And you'll get an A for trying."

He finished his drink and set down his empty glass, then began removing his clothes. Hoping this would be another failure for him, desperately wishing so, Nora went to one of the beds and turned down the spread and upper sheet. She took a long time doing it, dreading to face him again. When she turned, he was completely disrobed. With a sinking heart, she saw with revulsion the sagging of his flesh. But, too, she saw—and was even more impressed than before—the great size of him. Despite herself, she wondered what it would be like to be possessed by a man so huge. With the thought came self-disgust, and she strove to reach that state of aloofness she had promised herself to attain. He came to her, this great, gaunt man, and ran his hands over her. She unhooked her bra, freed her breasts, and he captured them, fondling them roughly. She removed her panties, closing her mind to the things his hands did to her. He drew her down onto the bed with him, and she lay supine and he on his side. Mercifully, she was able to force herself into a remoteness from it all and so she remained essentially untouched by his caresses.

After a time, he said plaintively, "It's no good. You'll have to help me. You know how?"

Nora knew how. She knew from the times when she had wanted Dave and he had been slow to be aroused. She turned toward the big old man and with her hands and lips tried to do what he was unable to accomplish for himself. She did all the mad, erotic things but in a numbed, mechanical way, striving to earn the vice-presidency for Dave. Yet Hammond's impotence refused to yield. At first she merely succeeded in doing what she did not want to do—arouse herself. She went from total lack of feeling to soaring passion and then to torment in the face of his continued inability.

Unleashed desire drove her to a frenzy. And suddenly, miraculously, her desire was communicated to him. He seized her by the shoulders and turned her roughly onto her back.

"Oh, yes—yes!" she gasped.

He came onto her, and she had to throttle a scream that rose in her throat with the hard jolt of his manhood. After that she moaned with the joyous sensation of passion accommodated and finally shrieked with the agonizing ecstasy of fulfillment.

Afterward, when he had removed himself from her, she lay at rest in the surcease of passion. Disgust came and it was entirely for herself. She had joined in the coupling of bodies with all her being and so she was to blame for her own degradation. I'm wanton, she thought; I deserve all the ugly things that happen to me. She felt that she should weep for herself but she was far beyond tears.

The man beside her had fallen into a deep sleep and his loud, asthmatic breathing rasped against her nerves. She got from the bed and snatched up her clothing, dressing with haste to hide her body. She got her purse from the bureau and, without really looking at herself in the mirror, touched up her lips and combed her hair. She walked quickly into the sitting room and closed the door behind her. She had not looked again at the sleeping man. She had no thought of waking him, even for reassurance that he would keep his promise.

She left the suite and the hotel. Reaching the street, she paused to orient herself, not knowing in which direction lay the parking lot where she had left her car. Finally she got her bearings and started walking. She walked fast, not like a person in a hurry to reach a pleasant destination but like one fleeing a feared pursuer. She was trying to run away from herself.

Driving directly home and seeing the house dark, she knew that Dave had not yet arrived. She ran the station wagon into the garage, then sat for a time with her arms folded on the steering wheel and her head resting on her arms. She simply wanted to die and wondered if she would ever rid herself of this nightmare feeling of self-disgust.

The ringing of the telephone summoned her out of the car and up to the kitchen where she spoke a toneless hello into the extension.

"Mrs. Osborne?" a voice said. "Mrs. David Osborne?"

"Yes."

"Mrs. Osborne, this is John Hadley at Camp Wee-ni- toka."

"Oh, yes, Mr. Hadley," she said, remembering him as the camp director. Then, alarm knifing through her: "Is something wrong? Is Louise ill?"

"She isn't ill, Mrs. Osborne, but I thought it best to call you. Louise has run away from camp. She's been gone since four o'clock this afternoon. That's six hours now, and I am, to say the least, becoming upset. I've been trying to reach you for the past two hours and—"

"Aren't you searching for her?" Nora cut in, her fear for Louise making her voice sound frantic.

"We are searching, Mrs. Osborne. I've called in the state police and have also gotten more than thirty volunteers to help. But we're having a severe electrical storm here and that makes looking for her difficult. I'd suggest that you and Mr. Osborne come up here as soon as possible."

"Why? Why did she run away?"

"It seems she had a quarrel with one of the other girls," the man said. "Will you come, Mrs. Osborne? The child will be frightened as well as unhappy when we do find her and we feel strongly that her parents should be here to comfort her."

"We'll be there," Nora said. "We'll leave right away."

We, she thought cradling the receiver. If only she could reach Dave ... She picked up the phone, dialed Penny's number and waited a long time but Penny did not answer. She would have to go alone. Oh, Dave—Dave! was her silent, anguished cry—the cry of a woman forsaken, who must face trouble with no one by her side.

She picked up her purse and car keys, returned to the garage and drove a dozen miles before the thought occurred to her that she could have left a note for Dave. But then, she told herself bleakly, he would not have found it. He would come home drunk and go to bed, never even noticing that she was not there.

CHAPTER SEVENTEEN

DAVE again spent the evening pub-crawling, trying to drown in liquor the constant, stinging awareness that his marriage was a shambles. He felt that nothing could ever repair the damage, not even his getting the vice-presidency. That Nora had given herself to Brandon Hoyt had cut him deeply and the hurt would be with him all his life. Her faithfulness, which he had never even thought to question, had always made him vastly proud, especially when he heard gossip about the extramarital flights of other men's wives.

But Nora's reason for having the affair with Hoyt had struck him an even harder blow. In effect, she had told him that she had little or no trust in his ability to give his family the security they deserved, so she had sought to help him by selling herself. Thereby she had destroyed his pride in himself as a man and even his self-confidence as a business executive.

She had ruined the fine thing their marriage had been but without accomplishing what she had set out to do. There had been no reason on earth for Nora to make a whore of herself, as she had so tragically done. By his own efforts alone, he would win the vice-presidency. The photostated letter was safe in his pocket. And on Monday morning at nine o'clock he would walk into Hoyt's office and give him an ultimatum:

"Either back me for the vice-presidency at the board meeting," Dave would say, "or I'll go to H. M. Forbes—or to Mark Hammond—with this."

Then he would show Hoyt the photostated copy of the man's own letter, offering to place an order if he could get a return.

So Dave would get the vice-presidency and his future with Worden-Forbes would be bright and assured. But that would not straighten out his marriage. Even if Nora threw herself into his arms and told him that he was an all-time wonder-boy, he would never be able to forget her lack of faith in his ability—nor her flagrantly degrading affair with Hoyt. Never could she salve the sickening hurt to his pride. Nothing could ever be the same between them.

Tonight he sat in a grubby midtown bar, the Barrel. He was on his fifth rye-on-the-rocks and the stuff was not doing a thing for him. If he could not soon find a way to forget the troubles of his marriage he felt that he would crack up. Hell, that would really be something—having a breakdown before getting a chance to face that Brandon Hoyt bastard.

Well, if whiskey would not give him forgetfulness, a woman might. That thought insinuated itself upon his mind and took a tenacious hold. He had not forgotten the night he had had Penny Austin. Maybe if he had her again … Well, why not? If Nora saw fit to sleep around, there was no reason why he should not do the same. One thing was certain: with Penny he would feel whole again in the manhood department. At least, for a little while.

He left his fifth drink barely touched, rose from his stool and walked steadily enough out to his car.

Fifteen minutes later he pulled into the Austin's driveway. He knew that Bart was in Dayton again and he hoped that no one else would be with Penny. There well could be someone, of course, for Penny was a real tramp. She could be with anybody. He switched off motor and lights, got from the Buick. He crossed the lawn to the door and pressed the bell button.

The outside light came on, the door opened and Penny frowned at him. "Oh, it's you. Well, what do you want?"

"You need to be told?" he asked, pushing the door farther open and stepping inside. "I want you, of course."

"Get out of here, Dave," Penny said flatly. "Go home to your wife. I don't want you. I've decided I don't like you even a little bit. You're a sulky, overgrown child. I'd feel I was robbing the cradle ever to have you again."

"Knock it off," he said, shutting the door. "If you're peeved because of what I said at the Florida Room, I apologize. Now come on—be nice."

He reached for her but she quickly sidestepped.

"I told you to go home to Nora," she said angrily. "She's the one who wants you—not I."

"There's never a time when you don't want a man, damn you I"

"Oh, yes there is. That time is right now. Get the hell out of here!"

He shook his head. "Not until I've had you," he said and moved toward her. "And I'm going to have you, even if I've got to rape you."

She backed away, looking frightened now as well as angry. Once across the entrance hall, she whirled and ran into the living room. She grabbed up the telephone and began dialing. He came and wrenched it from her hand.

"Who do you think you're calling?" he demanded.

"Nora, of course. Give it to me, Dave."

"No, I won't give it to you."

He put the phone down and grabbed her about the waist when she tried to pick up the phone. She whirled, struck at him with her fists. He jerked her off balance, forced her to the floor. He held her flat on her back with his left arm across her chest and his right leg across her legs. She fought fiercely to get free but was no match for him. He slipped his right hand under her skirt and forced it between her thighs. With the touch of his hand on her bare flesh, Penny abruptly stopped struggling.

"All right, you louse," she said. "But not here. Not on the floor, damn you!"

He held her for a while longer, not trusting her abrupt surrender. But the fight had gone out of her and now, as he caressed her thighs, she parted them so that he could touch the warm, nylon-sheathed nest there. She was ready and willing now, even eager.

'Where?"

"On the couch down in the rumpus room," she breathed.

"All right, come along," he said. He got to his feet and helped her rise.

She stared at him angrily for a moment, then turned and walked from the living room. Following, he saw that she was hastily unbuttoning her blouse …

Nora ran into the storm when still a dozen miles from Camp Wee-ni-toka. Traffic had been light and she had kept the car at an even, quiet seventy miles an hour. But now she was forced to cut her speed because the sluicing rain, which the windshield wipers could scarcely cope with, limited visibility. Lightning flashes slashed the darkness, each blinding chain followed by an ear-shattering thunderclap. Nora gripped the wheel until her fingers ached, frightened in spite of herself. She could not stop worrying about Louise, lost and panic-stricken in the fury of this storm … then Nora had to turn her full attention to guiding the station wagon along the narrow, tortuous mountain road.

Actually, Nora's fear for her daughter went farther than the image of the child, lost and alone in the storm. Her thoughts were haunted by something much worse that could have happened to Louise. Almost every day the newspapers carried stories of children falling into the hands of sex maniacs. Heaven help me, Nora thought, knowing the blame was hers. For she, rather than Dave, had believed that sending Louise to this summer camp would help them in their quest for higher status in the company hierarchy. And she, rather than Dave, had insisted that Louise stay on at Wee-ni-toka when the child had wanted to come home. Yes, this was one thing she could not blame on Dave.

She finally reached the little town of Pine Grove and Camp Wee-ni-toka was only two miles farther. However, the place was reached by a side road, made even more difficult in this storm than the road behind her. In running off, Nora reflected, Louise must certainly have planned, in her seven-year-old way, to go home. And she must have set out along this road, intending to get to Pine Grove and probably hitching a ride there to Lan- ford. Louise had been told always that she should never accept a ride from a stranger but under these circumstances, of course, she would have forgotten that. In her unhappiness, her desperation to get home, she would have seen no harm in accepting a lift.

She may have been picked up along this road, Nora thought. She may not have gotten even as far as Pine Grove and have been taken into the woods, into the thick growth of trees, dark and forbidding, that pressed down on either side of the road. Nora shuddered.

Brilliant blue-green lightning streaks, followed by crashing thunder, heralded stronger wind-swept torrents of rain. But now Nora's headlights showed her the stone pillars marking the entrance to Camp Wee-ni-toka. Another quarter mile and she saw the lighted windows of the administration building before which a dozen cars were parked, among them three state police cruisers.

Nora parked, got out and ran through the rain to the stone steps leading to the veranda. The door was opened before she reached it by Mrs. Hadley, the director's wife.

A dozen people were gathered inside the large living room, and all showed the same tense anxiety shared by those commonly touched by a grave emergency. A state trooper sat talking into a portable two-way radio but his frown showed that he was not receiving good news. Another trooper and two men in civilian clothes stood at a buffet table, eating sandwiches and drinking coffee. Each still wore a glistening wet slicker, so Nora knew that they had been out searching and intended to go again. The others in the room were women, members of the camp's staff. Louise's counselor, Miss Leland, came hurrying toward Nora, a look of distress on her rather plain face.

"I'm so sorry, Mrs. Osborne," she said in a rush of words. "I feel that it was my fault—I really do. If I'd paid more attention to Louise, I might have kept her from running away. But she told me she was tired and wanted to go to her cabin and rest until dinner. I gave her permission, of course. Then, when she didn't come to dinner, I went to her cabin. And she was gone."

"There's been no word about her at all?" Nora asked.

"None at all," Mrs. Hadley said. Stout and middle-aged, she was obviously distressed. "We know definitely that Louise did not go to the village. My husband and I went there as soon as we discovered that she was missing. The troopers checked later and no one at Pine Grove saw her. She must have gone into the woods, Mrs. Osborne. The men are searching there now, as they have been since shortly after six o'clock. Five troopers and most of the men from the village are looking for her, and the forest rangers have also been asked to help. If Louise isn't found by midnight, more men will come in."

The trooper at the radio was saying, "Nothing at that abandoned farmhouse, eh, Charlie? Okay. Stay with it."

The trooper and the two men at the buffet table bolted the last of their sandwiches, buttoned their raincoats and went out into the storm.

Then Miss Leland was again profusely apologizing for not having kept a closer watch on Louise. There had been a quarrel between Louise and a girl named Harriet Morton. Miss Leland had learned of it only after Louise had disappeared. Evidently that was the reason for the child's running off.

"If only she had told me about the quarrel," Miss Leland said miserably.

Mrs. Hadley said, "Come sit down, Mrs. Osborne. We'll have coffee. It may be a long wait, though 1 hope and pray that it won't be."

Nora let herself be led to a sofa but no sooner had she seated herself than she got up again, crossing the room to the trooper at the radio. He was young, capable looking, and she intuitively felt that he would know if there was a possibility that someone had taken Louise away.

"I'm Louise's mother," she said, "I'm worried that someone with—well, with criminal tendencies may have picked my daughter up. Do you think that has happened?"

"We've no reason to think it has, Mrs. Osborne."

"I'm awfully worried—frightened, really."

"That's understandable," he told her. "It's only natural to fear the worst. But there has been absolutely nothing like that—even molestations—reported in this area recently. We're assuming that your daughter is lost in the woods and we've no reason to think otherwise. She was upset over that quarrel with the other girl. Probably she brooded about it, then just wandered off."

"But shouldn't you people act on the possibility that she might have been picked up by someone? Why don't you set up road blocks?"

"We weren't notified of the child's disappearance until seven forty-five, Mrs. Osborne. By that time she had been gone for at least two hours, and possibly four hours. If some person had picked her up and taken her from this area, he's now long gone. Road blocks wouldn't catch him. If he didn't take her out of the area, we'll find him—and her. But for now it's better to act on the assumption that she's simply lost in the forest." He smiled at her. "You try to think that. Okay?"

"All right, I'll try." Nora smiled wanly, unreassured.

She returned to the sofa and sat there sipping the coffee Mrs. Hadley had brought her. Then, too upset to sit still, she asked if she could use the telephone.

"I wasn't able to reach my husband before I left home," she said. "He was at a—a business meeting. I'd like to try to get him now."

"Yes, of course," Mrs. Hadley said. "You can use the phone in my husband's office."

When the phone began to ring, Penny was lying in Dave's arms on the couch in her rumpus room. Dave and she had made vigorous, uninhibited love and then, exhausted, lay beside each other, silent and unmoving, until the emotional dullness of love-making's aftermath had dissipated itself. Still without words, they had turned to face each other and entwined their bodies in their approach to new passion. That they disliked each other intensely mattered not at all. For them mutual dislike and even anger served merely to heighten the enjoyment of the sexual act.

So, when the phone first rang, they were attempting to fan the embers of desire back into flame. Penny at first decided to ignore it, then, thinking that Bart might be calling, she broke away from Dave and moved through the darkness to the extension at the opposite side of the room. Picking up the phone, she was startled to hear Nora's voice:

"Penny, I'm calling from Louise's camp," Nora said. "Louise has run away. She's been gone since four o'clock this afternoon. The police are searching for her but there's a bad storm and—well, they haven't found her. Dave should be here. If he's with you, Penny, tell him to come—please."

And with that, Nora broke the connection.

Penny put down the phone and stood by it, badly shaken. How in heaven's name did Nora know about Dave and her? She felt guilty and ashamed.

From across the darkened room, Dave's voice, thick with whiskey and passion, called to her. "Come back here, you," he shouted.

"Dave, get up," she said. "Get up and get dressed."

"The hell I will."

She crossed the room to where her clothes lay in an untidy heap on the floor. She picked up the blouse and put it on.

"That was Nora." Her voice was flat. "She called from Louise's camp. Louise ran away and they can't find her. Nora wants you up there. Now get up, you louse, and get dressed. I'll have some black coffee ready for you by that time—so you can be halfway sober."

She put on her skirt and padded barefooted upstairs to the kitchen. She was pouring hot water onto the powdered coffee when Dave entered. He looked as though the frightening news had somewhat sobered him. He also looked as though someone had clobbered him. She was angry with him—as she was with herself, too, she had to admit—but she could be sympathetic.

"Drink it while it's hot," she said. "You've got a long drive ahead of you and you'd better be sober. I'd drive you, but—well, I just can't face Nora."

"How did she find out about us?"

"I don't know. Not from me."

"It's a mess," he said self-pityingly. "Everything's such a god-damn mess."

"Quit feeling sorry for yourself," Penny told him. "Worry about Louise—and Nora. That poor kid running away and get-ting lost."

He did not reply to that; he did not speak again. He drank the coffee, set down the empty cup, then turned to leave. She went to the door with him, watched him half run to his car and then drive away. She closed the door and leaned heavily against it.

For the first time in her life, Penny felt a disgust for sex, for the murky, devious byways, the cheap lies and shoddy intrigues that formed the lifeline of sexual unfaithfulness. She-had wanted to help Nora, not to hurt her. But even when trying to help her, she had probably hurt her in one or two ways: Tonight at the hotel cocktail lounge when she had pleaded a nonexistent engagement and had left Nora with Mark Hammond. Of course she had known the moment Mark had said he would like to see Nora that he would try to take her to bed. But also, of course, she had not known how Nora would react to old Mark's proposition. But now she did know, too late, that Nora would forever regret giving in to Mark, if she had really done so. Yet, if she had not given in, she would have spoiled Dave's last chance for the vice-presidency. So, reasoned Penny, she had hurt Nora, not helped her. And she had hurt her even more by having this silly but highly enjoyable affair with Dave.

The thought occurred to Penny that Dave and Nora were people essentially doomed to a tragic life. Basically decent people, they had been pushed into a world that destroys their kind. It would be better, Penny conjectured, if Dave did not get that vice-presidency; if he and Nora were forced to return to the dull, conventionally moralistic world that they were really a part of. It was a world that held lasting values for them—moral values actually as necessary to their lives as the oxygen in the air they breathed.

As for herself, Penny decided that she did not want sex in any form whatsoever for a long, long time. Her self-disgust was no small thing.

CHAPTER EIGHTEEN

NORA stood facing the big window, staring out into the rain-slashed blackness until her eyes ached. When, she wondered, would she have word of Louise?

Despite Nora's urgent pleas to join the other searching groups, the trooper at the walky-talky radio had ordered her to remain here. He had pointed out that the men had enough to do without looking after a distracted mother, unfamiliar with this rugged, wooded terrain. She would get lost, too.

"So you take it easy. We'll bring your little girl back in fine shape, Okay?"

Okay, Nora thought, nodding miserably. Sure. Great.

So she had waited, her heart jumping at every scratchy sound from the walky-talky receiver and no one had anything really to report. This area, that place, had been searched. Results: Negative. And Nora's knuckles were raw from striking the dusty window sill. Why, why did they not set up road blocks? Damn it, they should realize that every day little girls like Louise were horribly mutilated and killed by these sex maniacs. Right now the child might be lying out there, her clothes torn, her little body bloodily ravished, dead, the victim of one of these monsters. Nora's vision suddenly blinded her with tears.

Here she was, alone, in this place ...

When she saw the car's headlights searching up the roadway, she knew that Dave was coming to the camp. Then, as the headlights came closer, she felt a surge of jealous resentment rise in her, like a viciously clawing wild animal. Her mind was filled with a tape recording that constantly repeated: Penny and Dave ... Penny and Dave ...

Yet, when a tense-faced Dave opened the door and appeared with an extra raincoat over his arm and a flashlight in his hand, the sight of him made her heart ache. His face was so white and drawn that he looked as frightened as she felt. She hurried to him, clung to him.

"Oh, Dave, I've been so worried—so frightened."

"They haven't found—?"

"No," Nora said. "Not a trace." Then, hysteria threatening: "Dave, I'm so afraid someone has picked her up and—"

"Don't think it," he said. "We mustn't think such a thing."

She began to cry, at last giving way to painful sobbing and nothing Dave could say helped. Mrs. Hadley came quietly in and told him to take Nora to the office where they would be alone. She led them there, then left them.

Dave held Nora in his arms, letting her cry until, after a time, her sobbing quieted. She took the handkerchief from his breast pocket, wiped her eyes and blew her nose. Dave murmured what he hoped were comforting sounds, but she jerked away from him.

"We're being punished," she cried hysterically. 'We've done terrible things and now we're being punished. We've turned ourselves into awful people, just for the sake of—of belonging. I did wrong in forcing Louise to stay at this camp when she hated it. Children always sense what is wrong for them and Louise sensed that this camp was not right for her. She hasn't been happy since we moved to Wilshire Heights. And anyway, she left her friends in our old neighborhood and she misses them terribly. Dave, listen: we're trying to be what were not cut out to be. If something bad has happened to Louise I'll hate you and myself the rest of my life!"

Dave nodded, his face grave. "I understand how you feel, Nora," he said. "We have made a mess of our lives these past few months. I've got to go out there and find our daughter. Will you be all right alone?"

"I'll be all right alone," Nora said bitterly. "Haven't I been alone for a long while?"

He left, and in the main room he donned his raincoat. He ignored the advice of the trooper at the radio, which was not to go into the woods unless he was familiar with this wild country. Into the stormy night he went, crossing the wide clearing where the camp stood, then plunged in among the dense trees and undergrowth.

Afterward, he had no idea how far he tramped through the thick wet woodland in his frantic search for his daughter. He merely knew that he kept on the move the remainder of the night, wandering one way and another. Twice he encountered other searchers, small groups of weary men, and to them he identified himself as Louise's father but learned that no one had found any trace of the child. He continued to go it alone and was surprised to find how quickly he tired. Then he realized that his heavy drinking and his love-making with Penny had sapped his endurance. But he had no thought of giving up.

He stopped every few minutes to call his daughter's name, waited hopefully for an answer and then, failing to hear one, pressed on. The beam of his flashlight lanced into dark gullies, among clusters of rock, into a deep ravine. And despite legs that were leaden with weariness and laboring lungs, he persisted in his search through this night of storm.

He came finally to the weed-grown road which Nora and Louise and he had crossed on their trek last Sunday. He recalled how happy the three of them had been for a little while as Nora told her little story of the Indian family finding the place which Louise had named the Secret Cave.

Abruptly, Dave felt his heart leap with sudden hope.

Louise would not have forgotten that place, which had touched off her imagination as well as Nora's. A child's mind magnifies such small incidents, he told himself, and retains them forever as cherished memories. In running away, Louise would have realized the impossibility of her reaching home. But she would have had some refuge in mind. That might have been the Secret Cave, which, in Nora's fantasy, had been the refuge of the Indian family in a fierce storm like this one.

Suddenly Dave knew that his daughter was there. She would be huddled under the rocky ledge, sheltered from the storm and safe in every other way. Sheltered and safe, but undoubtedly as frightened at being alone in the stormy darkness as any seven-year-old would be.

Dave drove himself on, across the road and into the dense woodland just as the rain stopped and the sky began to turn gray with approaching dawn. He did not come to the place he sought, however, because he had not crossed the road at the same point where Louise and Nora and he had crossed last Sunday. Again he wandered one way and another, pausing often to call his daughter's name. He began to think that he would not be able to find the Secret Cave, that he would have to stop and turn back for other searchers to help him. He did stop but tried calling out once more. And this time he thought he heard a faint answering call.

He shouted more loudly: "Louise! Louise, baby!"

And, yes, there was again a faint answer.

Running in the direction from which the answering call seemed to come, he tripped over a root. His forward momentum carried him through a tangle of brush and then he plummeted down a steep slope. He sprawled at the base of the slope, dazed and in pain. His head hurt and there was a knife-sharp ache in his left side. When he picked himself up after several minutes, he felt an even greater pain in his left ankle. He was barely able to endure the sharp stabbing hurt when he put his weight on his left foot. Halting to rest, he called out once more.

This time he knew that it was Louise who answered. "Daddy—Daddy!" she called.

Minutes later he made his painful way out of the trees to the small clearing by the bluff in which the Secret Cave was located. Louise stood in the hollow at the base of the bluff, her hair disheveled and her blue denim camp uniform wet and bedraggled. But she was alive and unharmed and Dave sobbed with vast relief.

She came running to him, crying happily, "I knew you'd come, Daddy! Where's Mother? Didn't she come with you?"

Dave caught her up in his arms, too choked with feeling to answer at once. He could only mutter, "Thank God! Oh, thank God!"

Though Louise was in better physical shape than he was, Dave insisted upon carrying her but after a short distance he was forced to stop and put her down. He leaned against a tree trunk and gently felt his sore ankle, which he found badly swollen. The throbbing pain was agonizing even when he was not placing his weight upon that foot. Too, since carrying Louise, the sharp ache in his left side was more severe.

"I fell and hurt myself, honey," he said. "You think you can walk the rest of the way?"

"Oh, sure," Louise said. "I'm fine. Or I will be if you take me home. Will you take me home, Daddy?"

"You bet your boots I'll take you home."

Louise giggled. "I'm not wearing boots, you silly." Then, anxiously: "Are you mad at me because I ran away?"

"No, I'm not mad, baby. But you shouldn't have done it."

"Well, a girl called me names. She said I was—"

"You forget it," Dave told her. "It's over now, and you're going home. But first, we'll have to find our way back to the camp."

"Find our way?" Louise said, her eyes grown round. Are we lost?"

Dave laughed despite his pain. "No, not really," he said.

He took her by the hand and, limping badly, walked with her through the dense woods. He began to think he would not be able to return to the camp. The pain in his ankle was becoming unbearable.

They had traveled perhaps a half-mile when they heard a voice calling the child's name.

"Listen, Daddy," she said, surprised. "Somebody's calling me. Isn't that strange?"

"It's strange, all right," he said, smiling. "You call back, eh?"

As Louise called, "Hello, hello, who are you?" Dave sank to the ground and sat with his back to a tree trunk. His ankle was swollen to twice normal size and throbbed with pain even now.

A trooper and four civilian searchers emerged from the surrounding trees and brush. They moved slowly, weary from spending the night tramping through the forest. But they managed to grin at sight of Louise and to show surprise at seeing her father with her.

"So it took a greenhorn to find her, eh, Mr. Osborne?" the trooper said. Then, to Louise: "Hiya, honey. How are you feeling?"

"I'm fine," Louise said. "But my daddy's hurt. I guess it's lucky you came along. He needs help to get back to the camp."

Dave did need help. He required a stretcher to bear him back to Camp Wee-ni-toka, the attention of a doctor summoned from Pine Grove, and a state police car to take him to the hospital at Lanford. There he found that his head and his side were not seriously injured, but the X-ray showed a fractured bone in his ankle. The ankle went into a cast, and Dave into a hospital bed.

For her mother, Louise's return alive and unharmed seemed a miracle, and the ordeal of that stormy night brought Nora to make a momentous decision. After stopping at the hospital with Dave's pajamas, robe and toilet kit she started home with Louise. And at that time she made up her mind about the future of the Osborne family.

She needed still more time to think things out and she concentrated on her plan the remainder of the day. That night she lay awake for hours, pondering how she would tell Dave tomorrow.

Nora drove Louise to Sunday school in the morning, then returned home and called a sitter, a college girl she trusted, to stay with the child while she went on to the hospital. Picking Louise up at eleven o'clock, she told her about the sitter. Louise fussed a little, saying that she, too, wanted to visit her father.

"I've something to talk over with Daddy," Nora told her. "Something important."

"Something too important for me to hear?"

"That's right, darling," Nora said, laughing.

She was surprised that she was able to laugh, for she felt so-so grim. But maybe her ability to laugh again was proof, she reflected, that her decision was the right one. She merely had to make Dave see how important her course of action would be to all of them.

The sitter came at one-thirty, and Nora left in the station wagon a few minutes later. After parking at the hospital, she sat in the car for a moment, mentally rehearsing what she would say to Dave.

She must make two points clear to him. One, she could no longer put up with their estrangement. He would have to forgive and forget her affair with Brandon Hoyt, and she would forgive and forget his with Penny Austin. Being a party to a halfway marriage was an impossible role for her to take. The second point was that she no longer wanted to be a part of the group in which they now moved. If dropping out meant that Dave would have to resign from Worden-Forbes, then that was all right with her. If he would not give in, she would have no recourse but to consider a divorce.

That was what she had decided, and she intended to give Dave that ultimatum. If she was wrong in believing that he still loved her and wanted to keep their marriage intact, she would take Louise and leave him. She would not go on being what she had become. The price they were paying for belonging was far, far too high.

Tears came but she blinked them away and left the station wagon, walked purposefully into the hospital and took the elevator to the fifth floor. But while going along the corridor to Dave's room, she found that her nerve was failing her. She began to doubt that she could go through with her plan. The trouble was, she was too deeply in love with Dave.

He was out of bed and learning to use a pair of crutches.

He gave her an uncertain smile. "How am I doing?"

"You're doing fine, Dave."

"I'll be on these things quite a while," he said. He moved awkwardly to the bed. He seated himself on its edge, then asked, "How is Louise?"

"She's all right. She went to Sunday school this morning.

"And how are you feeling?"

"Not happy."

"Neither am I," he said. "Sit down. I want to talk."

"So do I want to talk," she replied. "And I'd better stay on my feet to say my piece."

He gazed at her bleakly. "Well, go ahead. Get it off your chest."

She shook her head. "You first," she said realizing that her nerve was just about wholly gone.

He fumbled in the pockets of his robe, brought out a cigarette. He didn't speak until he'd lit it and then he searched for words.

"I don't know how to say it, Nora, without seeming to be placing the blame on you. But it's this way: I became involved with Penny because I was sick with jealousy. And because my pride was hurt. I never really wanted her. I don't even like her. I guess I was acting like a kid trying to get even."

'So you got even."

"And I hurt you," he said bitterly. "One of the two people I love. But, damn it, you shouldn't have given yourself to Brandon Hoyt—even if you thought it would get me the vice-presidency. It was a lousy thing to happen to a man in love."

"And now you're no longer in love with me?"

"I didn't say that. I am in love with you—I always will be. But I don't like what you've become—or what I've become."

"You're echoing my words, Dave. You know that, don't you?"

He nodded. "I know. But I made up my own mind about things. Nora, I want out. I'm not going on with Worden-Forbes, even as a vice-president. And I don't care to be a part of the crowd we're associating with. I want to make a clean break."

Now you're echoing what I've been wishing, Nora thought. Aloud, she said, "You mean you want to resign from the company?"

"Yes."

"And have to start all over?"

"I can go to work right away for Triton Electronics. Bill Marsten will pay me nine thousand a year. Of course, that's not nearly what I'm getting at Worden- Forbes and we'd have to move out of Wilshire Heights. But I won't do it unless you agree. If you won't agree, I'll go after that vice-presidency. Oh, I know you doubt that I can get it, with Hoyt backing that Air Force general. But I was telling the truth when I said that I had something on him."

He explained about the photostat of the letter he had gotten from Harvey Ward, then continued. "I won't be able to see Hoyt tomorrow because of my ankle. But I can just as easily lay it on the line for him over the phone."

Nora sank weakly into the bedside chair feeling utterly jolted. So Dave's talk had not been mere boyish bragging, after all. He actually did have a way to force Brandon Hoyt to back him. What a fool she had been to think that he was incapable of getting and holding this top job. How stupid she had been to hurt him by her traipsing from bed to bed, honestly thinking that she could help him by acting like a cheap little whore. She had let herself be used and degraded by three different men and all to no purpose. If Dave should ever find out about Mark Hammond, God help her!

"The strange thing is," Dave went on, "I could have settled this with Hoyt days ago. I kept putting off getting in touch with him. I didn't know why I kept stalling until this thing happened to Louise. That opened my eyes to what a mess both of us have made of our marriage. I hate Brandon Hoyt for having had you in bed, Nora, but when I face it, I know I wouldn't get any real, honest satisfaction by forcing him to back us. That suddenly struck me as a lousy way to get a promotion. Damn it, I guess I'm just not cut out to be a good blackmailer. Hell, I don't even want that silly vice-presidency now. But if you're set on holding onto the house in Wilshire Heights and being part of the crowd—well, I'll call him. And clobber him with that photostat."

Nora's voice was husky and her eyes brimming as she turned to him. "Anything you want to do, darling, is just what I want, too."

"Better give me a signed memo on that," Dave grinned. "Some day you might forget what you've just said."

"I won't Dave. Cross my heart, honest and truly. Know why? Because what you've decided is exactly the same thing that I had made up my mind to since the first day you were in the hospital. I'd planned to tell you that I don't want you to keep on at Worden-Forbes. That crowd is just no good for us, Dave, and the price we've been paying for all this plushy kind of life is too high. Nothing is worth all the heartache it costs."

They gazed at each other wonderingly for a brief moment and in the flash of time each had the same thought. Nora got from her chair at the same instant that Dave adjusted his crutches and got from the bed. He hobbled to her and, balanced on his crutches, put his hands to her waist. Nora's arms were about his neck, and their lips met, gently at first then opening with the long-missed fire of their love and passion.

After they had kissed, Nora whispered, "Darling, how long will they keep you here away from me?"

"Until tomorrow morning," Dave said. "Can you wait?"

"Hardly. Can you?"

"Hell, no," he grinned.

"Well, neither can I," Nora smiled softly, that smouldering glow coming into her eyes. "But isn't there anything that we can do about it?"

A slender young brown-haired nurse silently entered the room at that moment. Her eyes twinkled as she answered Nora's question. "Not one blessed thing can you do," she said. "And isn't it a crying shame!"

THE END